PRAISE FOR DONNA GRANT'S
BEST-SELLING ROMANCE NOVELS

"A breathtaking tale...I absolutely loved it!"
—Romance Junkies on Dark Craving, Dark Kings Series

"The author has created a fantastic and mesmerizing fantasy world with intriguing twists, surprises and unique elements that keeps the reader turning the pages to the very end."
—Night Owl Reviews on Dark Heat, Dark Kings Series

"Evie and Malcolm is a couple that makes it impossible not to love them."
—The Jeep Diva, Dark Warriors Series

"Grant's smoldering seventh Dark Warrior outing will grip readers from the first page, immersing them in her wounded, lonely couple's journey of redemption...each scene is filled with Grant's clever, complex characters and trademark sizzle."
—Romantic Times Magazine (RT Book Reviews), Dark Warriors Series

DON'T MISS THESE OTHER NOVELS
BY NYT & USA TODAY BESTSELLING AUTHOR DONNA GRANT

CONTEMPORARY PARANORMAL

DRAGON KINGS SERIES

(Spin-off series from DARK KINGS)

Book 1: Dragon Revealed (novella)

Book 2: Dragon Mine

Book 3: Dragon Unbound (novella)xxx

REAPER SERIES

Book 1: Dark Alpha's Claim

Book 2: Dark Alpha's Embrace

Book 3: Dark Alpha's Demand

Books 1-3 Bundle: Tall Dark Deadly Alpha

Book 4: Dark Alpha's Lover

Book 5: Dark Alpha's Night

Book 6: Dark Alpha's Hunger

Book 7: Dark Alpha's Awakening

Book 8: Dark Alpha's Redemption

Book 9: Dark Alpha's Temptation

Book 10: Dark Alpha's Caress

Book 11: Dark Alpha's Obsession

Book 12: Dark Alpha's Need

Book 13: Dark Alpha's Silent Night

Book 14: Dark Alpha's Passion

DARK KINGS SERIES

Book 0.1: Dark Craving

Book 0.2: Night's Awakening

Book 0.3: Dawn's Desire

Books 0.1-0.4 Bundle: Dark Heat

Book 1: Darkest Flame

Book 2: Fire Rising

Book 3: Burning Desire

Book 4: Hot Blooded

Book 5: Night's Blaze

Book 6: Soul Scorched

Book 6.5: Dragon King (novella)

Book 7: Passion Ignites

Book 8: Smoldering Hunger

Book 9: Smoke and Fire

Book 9.5: Dragon Fever (novella)

Book 10: Firestorm

Book 11: Blaze

Book 11.5: Dragon Burn (novella)

Book 11.6: Constantine: A History, Part 1

Book 12: Heat (short story)

Book 12.5: Constantine: A History, Part 2 (short story)

Book 13: Torched

Book 13.1: Constantine: A History, Part 3 (short story)

Book 13.5: Dragon Night (novella)

Book 14: Dragonfire

Book 14.5: Dragon Claimed (novella)

Book 15: Ignite

Book 16: Fever

Book 16.5: Dragon Lost (novella)

Book 17: Flame

Book 18: Inferno

Book 19: Whisky and Wishes, A Dark Kings Special Holiday Novella

Book 20: Heart of Gold, A Dark Kings Special Valentine's Novella

Book 21: Of Fire and Flame

Book 22: A Dragon's Tale (Bundle of Books 19, 20, & 21)

The Dragon King Coloring Book

Dragon King Special Edition Character Coloring Book: Rhi

DARK WARRIORS SERIES

Book 1: Midnight's Master

Book 2: Midnight's Lover

Book 3: Midnight's Seduction

Book 4: Midnight's Warrior

Book 5: Midnight's Kiss

Book 6: Midnight's Captive

Book 7: Midnight's Temptation

Book 8: Midnight's Promise

Book 8.5: Midnight's Surrender (novella)

CHIASSON SERIES

Book 1: Wild Fever

Book 2: Wild Dream

Book 3: Wild Need

Book 4: Wild Flame

Book 5: Wild Rapture

THE ROYAL CHRONICLES NOVELLA SERIES

Book 1: Prince of Desire

Book 2: Prince of Seduction

Book 3: Prince of Love

Book 4: Prince of Passion

Books 1-4: The Royal Chronicles Box Set

Mystic Trinity (a series connecting novel)

Dark Beginnings: A First in Series Boxset

Chiasson Series, Book 1: Wild Fever

LaRue Series, Book 1: Moon Kissed

The Royal Chronicles Series, Book 1: Prince of Desire

MILITARY ROMANCE / ROMANTIC SUSPENSE

SONS OF TEXAS SERIES

Book 1: The Hero

Book 2: The Protector

Book 3: The Legend

Book 4: The Defender

Book 5: The Guardian

COWBOY / CONTEMPORARY

HEART OF TEXAS SERIES

Book 1: The Christmas Cowboy Hero

Book 2: Cowboy, Cross My Heart

Book 3: My Favorite Cowboy

Book 4: A Cowboy Like You

Book 5: Looking for a Cowboy

Book 6: A Cowboy Kind of Love

STAND ALONE BOOKS

That Cowboy of Mine

Home for a Cowboy Christmas

Mutual Desire

Forever Mine

Savage Moon

Check out Donna Grant's Online Store at

www.DonnaGrant.com/shop

for autographed books, character themed goodies, and more!

DARK ALPHA'S NEED

REAPERS, BOOK 12

DONNA GRANT

This is a work of fiction. All of the characters, organizations, and events portrayed in this novel are either products of the author's imagination or are used fictitiously.

www.DonnaGrant.com
www.MotherofDragonsBooks.com

DEDICATION

To Teresa K.

Thank you for the time and love you've devoted to the Dark World.

CHAPTER ONE

Sly Stag Pub
Dublin

Nothing about the mellow music drifting from the speakers calmed Torin. He hadn't been able to shake the dark feeling hanging over him since Rordan's last mission. Something wicked was coming, and for the first time since becoming a Reaper, he was worried.

Torin sat at the bar, his gaze moving across every face in the tavern. The Fae Others were targeting Reapers. He and his brethren wouldn't stand by and wait for the Others to find them. No, the Reapers were going after the bastards—on Death's orders.

His gaze met those of his fellow Reaper, Aisling, across the bar. Her long, black and silver hair hung down her back in dozens of small plaits. She wrapped her fingers with their long, red nails around her glass. Her disinterest in those around her had males and females alike doing everything they could to get her attention. Aisling lifted the glass of whisky to her lips and took a long drink before winking at him, even as a female Light rubbed her breasts against Aisling's arm.

Torin hid his smile and gave a slight shake of his head. They weren't here for fun. They were at the Sly Stag to find someone. Being out among so many Fae—both Dark and Light—was dangerous for them now. Once, the Reapers had been dismissed as monsters that Fae children's parents used to keep them in line.

The Reapers had hidden in plain sight for centuries, walking among Fae and humans alike without anyone the wiser. When they became Reapers, they left their lives, families, and friends behind, allowing everyone to believe they had died. Secrecy was imperative. Death made sure of that because she had foreseen that some might take advantage of knowing a Reaper.

Torin finished off the last of his ale and leaned his arm on the bar as he shifted sideways to look at those behind him. This wasn't the only Fae pub in Dublin. There were others in the heart of the tourist area where mortals walked in without realizing just what type of establishment it was.

Fae had mingled with humans since first coming to the realm. Some Fae—as well as a few Druids—had created certain places that were deemed neutral ground so the Dark and Light Fae, as well as *drough* and *mie* Druids, could mingle without fear of being attacked. The Sly Stag was such an establishment. Torin had visited it before becoming a Reaper. He hadn't liked it then.

He didn't like it now.

If the Fae Council came to fruition, they wouldn't need places like the Sly Stag. Light and Dark had been getting along fine in neutrally defined pubs for eons. They could get along outside of them, too.

Well. Most could.

The bartender caught Torin's eye and jerked his chin toward the door. Torin's gaze fell on the Dark female as she came to a halt just after entering. Her gaze darted around quickly as if searching for someone.

Or hiding.

When she ducked into one of the back hallways, Torin knew she was hiding. From what, was the question. He slid his gaze to Aisling to find that his fellow Reaper had seen their target, as well. Torin tossed money onto the bar to pay for his drink and walked to where the Dark had gone. Aisling untangled the Light Fae from her arm and made her way toward the other hallway.

This wasn't the first tip they had tracked down in an effort to find the Others. Fae everywhere were talking about the group, many touting that they were involved when, in fact, they weren't.

The original Others had been comprised of a *drough* and *mie* Druid from another realm, a *mie* and *drough* Druid from Earth, and a Light and Dark Fae. The six had combined their powers to wipe out the Dragon Kings and take over Earth to claim the magic. Ultimately, the Dragon Kings had triumphed, though it had been close. The Reapers had joined in to help the Kings defeat the Others. When the Others were all gone, everyone believed the threat was over. Unfortunately, the Fae, as well as a group of Druids, were attempting to form their own factions.

Torin was ready to find the Dark female and get whatever information she had—if she had any at all. He wasn't optimistic after so many failed missions. On top of it all, they had to keep an eye out for the Fae Others, who were most likely trying to track the Reapers and do away with them.

The hallway made a U, complete with private rooms. Light and Dark lovers often met there for dalliances they didn't want their kind to learn about. The rooms were locked with magic, preventing anyone but those renting them from entering. Thankfully, that didn't stop Torin and Aisling from finding their target.

Death, whose real name was Erith, was a goddess. She only had two requirements for someone to become a Reaper: they had to be skilled warriors, and each of them had to have been betrayed—the betrayals leading to their deaths or murders. Erith would come to them right before their last breath and offer them a second chance as a Reaper to do her bidding without question or fail.

Upon acceptance, Death gave a tiny portion of her power to enhance what each already had. A Fae could veil themselves for seconds at a time. A Reaper could veil themselves indefinitely. Their magic also exceeded that of any other individual Fae. The Others combined their magic, which was why the Reapers were concerned.

Erith was the judge and jury for all Fae. She decided when it was time to reap a soul, and that's when she sent the Reapers. It was Death who kept the balance within the Fae. Disrupting that in any way could have dire consequences.

Torin waited until he was in the hallway alone before veiling himself. The Fae could teleport into the pub but not into the rooms. It was done to guarantee the privacy of those renting the spaces. However, that didn't stop a Reaper.

He jumped into each room, searching for the target until he finally found her in the back corner. To his surprise, she was alone on the bed with her back pressed against the headboard, staring at the door as if she expected someone to come through it at any second. Her black and silver hair hung past her shoulders and draped over one side to show that the lower half was shaved. To his amusement, he spotted silver stud earrings in the shape of mushrooms. She wore a white tank top beneath an oversized dark gray sweatshirt that hung off one shoulder. The sleeves were rolled at the cuff and pushed haphazardly up both arms to reveal several bracelets on each wrist, varying from beads to silver and gold. Black jeans were tucked into knee-high biker boots, complete with silver buckles at the ankles.

She had a classic, delicate beauty that unnerved him. Her large eyes were framed with thick lashes and gently arching eyebrows. Her high cheekbones seemed to have a sheen that made them stand out even more. Her full lips were a deep mauve color. She was unbelievably stunning.

The longer Torin watched her, the deeper his frown grew, and the more rattled he became—though he couldn't discern why. He stayed until Aisling appeared. As another added benefit of Erith's powers, Reapers could see each other while veiled. They couldn't, however, speak, or they would be heard.

Aisling jerked her head to the side, motioning for Torin to jump back into the hallway so they could talk. He found himself hesitating after Aisling left. Something about this Dark female didn't sit right with him. It could be her fear. It was so obvious, he could almost reach out and touch it.

"About damn time," Aisling said when he met her in the hallway with their veils dropped.

Torin glanced at the door that led to the room. "What do you think of her?"

"I think I'm tired of spying on people."

Torin jerked his head to Aisling, her quip not what he'd expected. "What?"

"Nothing," she said with a shake of her head. "She looks petrified."

"Aye."

"Want me to talk to her?"

Torin thought about that for a moment. "She might respond better to you."

"But?" Aisling asked, her brows raised.

"I don't know. There's just something…off…about her."

Aisling rolled her eyes. "Here we go again."

"I know what you're thinking, but it isn't going to happen."

She snorted. "You, Balladyn, and I are the only Reapers who haven't found our mates. The last time I went on a mission with Cathal, he found Sorcha. He also kept saying there was something about her."

"I'm not Cathal, and I'm not looking for anything."

"Yeah, well, it doesn't matter if you're looking or not. When love comes, it'll knock you off your feet whether you're prepared or not."

Torin studied Aisling. They all had pasts. Once they became Reapers, they were no longer Light or Dark. They did, however, keep the coloring of their former lives. Aisling had been a Dark Fae. She never spoke of her past. Hell, none of them did. But if the nightmares she had meant anything, then she had one hell of a former life that hadn't loosened its hold.

Yet, he didn't think her comment about love had anything to do with her past. In fact, he suspected it had something to do with Xaneth, though Aisling would probably never admit to it. She, even more than Death, was intent on finding the royal Light Fae who had been tortured by his aunt and Queen of the Light, Usaeil.

Aisling put her hands on her hips and sighed as she looked around. "Stop it."

"Stop what?" Torin asked, frowning.

"Looking at me like I might fall to pieces any second," she answered as she glared at him with her red eyes.

Torin bowed his head in acknowledgement. "We might not be blood, but we're family. We look out for each other. Always."

"You think I don't know that?" she asked, a tinge of anger in her voice.

"I think we all need to be reminded that we aren't in this alone. That we have others to lean on."

"I've always been alone, Torin. I've only ever been able to depend on myself—until Erith offered me a position as a Reaper. Death may have found us, but it was Eoghan who brought us together."

Torin smiled, thinking of that day. "We've survived so much. We'll get through this."

"First, we need to see what information, if any, our target has."

"I've a feeling she won't open the door."

Aisling twisted her lips. "We can't wait for her to come out."

"She's hiding."

"Then we need to find out who she's running from. Or…we can jump into the room and alert her to who we are."

Torin ran a hand down his face. "We don't have time to wait."

"Nope."

"Fek," he murmured.

Aisling shrugged and knocked on the door.

Torin glared at her.

She smiled, shooting him a sassy look.

Time stretched as the target within didn't utter a sound.

Aisling knocked again. Then, in her best helpless voice, she said, "Hello? Is this room open? I'm trying to get away from someone. All the others are occupied."

Torin turned to lean against the wall, crossing his arms over his chest when the target still didn't reply.

Aisling threw up her hands in defeat.

Torin really didn't want to teleport into the room. He didn't want anyone to know about the Reapers, not to mention, the female could start screaming. Or she could attack them. Neither option was viable. But neither could they wait her out. If she had information, they needed it.

Immediately.

And if she knew who the Reapers were, then she was already dead. Death didn't let anyone who wasn't part of the Reapers know of them and live—unless there were special circumstances and very good reasons.

Torin dropped his arms and turned to Aisling.

"I tried," she whispered.

That only left one choice.

CHAPTER TWO

What the fek had she gotten herself into? Breda pulled her knees up
to her chest and dropped her face into her hands. Stupid. That's
what she was. Utterly stupid. And it was going to get her killed.

She dropped her head back against the headboard and looked
out at the room. Dim lights in the ceiling pointed to the red leather
sofa on the opposite side of the space. The walls were black and
accented with black crown molding. The floor was black tile with a
large, red and black rug spread over it. Crimson satin covered the
large four-poster bed, and black bindings hung from each of the
corners.

The room was made for lovers. It wasn't a place she could stay
indefinitely. But, at the moment, she had nowhere else to go.

"So fekking stupid," she said to herself.

At least, the walls were soundproof. She didn't want to know
what was going on in the rooms around her.

Her eyes snapped to the door when someone knocked. Breda's
heart slammed into her ribs, knocking against them in a chaotic
cadence. The female voice that reached her did little to calm her
nerves.

Had they found her? Already?

Breda's mind raced to find a way out of the Sly Stag and Ireland, although she knew they would find her no matter where she was on this realm. If only she could go to another realm to escape. She'd had narrow calls before, but she knew there was no getting away this time. Because once they found her, they would inflict unimaginable agony upon her—for centuries.

Another knock sounded. This time, the voice asked for help. Breda hoped the woman wasn't really in trouble because nothing would get her to open the door. Humans liked to call it fight or flight, and she was absolutely in flight mode.

No sooner did that thought go through her mind than a man and woman appeared in her room. Breda instantly jerked back, though there was no place for her to go since she was already pressed tightly against the headboard. Her gaze moved from the Dark female to the Light male. Neither looked like soldiers, but the fact that they had gotten into the room when they shouldn't have been able to, meant they were either from the Others or they were…Reapers.

Either way, she was fekked.

Her stomach clenched in dread.

"Hi," the woman said as she tilted her head of black and silver braids that fell to her waist. She wore a black moto jacket with a red shirt beneath, paired with black jeans that had rips at the knees, along with the most beautiful pair of combat boots Breda had ever seen. "We were hoping you'd open the door so we could talk."

"We only want to ask you a few questions," the man said.

Breda's gaze moved to him. He was tall and broad-shouldered, wearing more subdued attire—a black tee showcasing his impressive build, denim, and black boots. His shoulder-length black hair was longer on top and shoved to the side as if he had run his hands through it. Something about his silver eyes held her ensnared.

The more she gazed into the beautiful orbs, the calmer she became. She frowned, thinking he was using magic, but she felt nothing. He was clean-shaven, his rugged looks catching her attention from his jawline to the intense way he watched her.

It took everything Breda had to pull her eyes from him. She returned her gaze to the female. "How did the two of you get in?"

"That doesn't matter," the woman said.

Breda snorted. "I beg to differ."

"There isn't a place we *can't* get into," the male answered.

The woman snapped her head to him, shooting him a glare. Breda watched the exchange with interest. She glanced at the male again, not allowing herself time to linger over his handsome face. Just a few seconds ago, Breda had thought her heart would burst from her chest, she was so scared. Now, she was asking questions. What the hell was going on?

The woman blew out a breath and looked to Breda once more. "As we said, we have questions."

"So?" Breda said, realizing then that she was with two very powerful Fae. "I'm not answering anything."

The man took a step toward her. "You're hiding. My guess is from the Others."

Breda's stomach dropped to her feet. They were blocking the door, preventing her from leaving. Her blood ran like ice through her veins. She slipped from the bed, getting to her feet and prepared to fight. If they weren't soldiers from the Others, then they were, in fact…Reapers.

Fek. Fekfekfekfekfekfekfekfekfek.

"Easy," the male said as he lifted his hands, palms out in front of him. "We're not here to hurt you."

The woman moved to the sofa and sat, crossing one leg over the other. She drummed her long, red nails against the leather. "He's right. In fact, we could be the ones who save you."

Breda shot both a dubious look. "You actually expect me to trust you two? Do I look like a fool?"

"You look like a woman at the end of her rope with a long drop below you," the female stated in a dry tone.

The man lowered his arms after frowning at the woman. He caught Breda's gaze. "You're right. You have no reason to trust us, and we have no reason to trust you."

"You're the ones who came into a locked room," Breda pointed out. "A room, I might add, that no one is supposed to be able to teleport into."

The woman quirked a brow. "I'm only going to say this once. We're not with the Others."

Breda barely bit back a reply. She wanted to believe them, if only because she might not be alone in this. And she really didn't want to be alone. But if she went down that road, she was setting herself up to be betrayed. Besides, wanting to ask her questions didn't mean they were going to help. Likely, it was the opposite.

If only she could believe they were Reapers, then she might take a chance with them. Yet, a doubt lingered in her mind. Hearing the Reapers were real didn't mean they were. And she knew for a fact that the Others and their soldiers were very, very real. Which meant, the two in her room had to be from them.

Breda didn't have formal battle training, but she knew enough to stay alive. Her best chance was getting to the door and then the nearest Fae doorway as fast as she could. It would be a long shot. The female looked bored, but Breda wasn't fooled. The woman had her entire attention focused on Breda. And the man, well…Breda didn't want to think about him.

She quickly went through the few scenarios of getting to the door. None of them were good, and most ended with her capture. That simply wouldn't do. She would rather die than be brought back to the Others alive. She knew what happened to the Fae the soldiers went after, and she wasn't going to be one of them.

Just as Breda started to dash for the door, a scream rent the air from within the pub. A second later, there were more. It was so loud, it penetrated the soundproof walls.

"Shite," the woman said as she jumped to her feet. "We've got to go."

"Not yet," the man said.

The female rolled her eyes and disappeared. Breda glanced at the exit. There was a chance she could get around him and make it to the door, but would she be able to open it? And what would be in

the hall when she did? She knew those terrified screams. It meant
the soldiers had found her.

The woman returned and looked to the man. "It's them. A
group is checking every female in the pub. There's another kicking
in doors. We've got seconds until they reach this room."

The man's head swung to her. Breda backed into the corner at
his penetrating look. She couldn't fight these two and the soldiers.
Then again, if she attacked the couple, perhaps they would kill her.
It would be a mercy if the soldiers couldn't get a hold of her.

The man started toward her.

"You've got to be kidding," the woman said through clenched
teeth.

Breda lifted her hands and released magic. The man deflected
the balls of power with ease. Before she could get off another orb,
he was upon her, moving so close he had her pressed into the
corner. She had to tilt her head back to look at his face.

"Not a word," he ordered in a deadly tone. "Not a single
syllable."

"This is madness," the woman said as she joined them.

To Breda's utter shock, the two stood in front of her as they
faced the door. Each of them wrapped their fingers around one of
her wrists. She thought it was to prevent her from getting away.
When two soldiers kicked open the door and stormed inside, Breda
expected a battle. Instead, nothing happened.

The woman turned her head to Breda and put her finger to her
lips. Breda's breathing was ragged, her nerves stretched to the
limit. She began shaking the longer the soldiers were in the room.
The man's hand tightened on her a millisecond before the two
soldiers exchanged a glance. They raised their hands. When they
did, the man turned to Breda as the woman vanished. Breda
parted her lips, but he put his hand over her mouth as a scream
bubbled up.

With her next breath, she found herself in a field. The man
released her. Breda stumbled back several steps, glancing around her
to see nothing but some trees and the vast night sky. Her chest
heaved, the screams of those within the pub still ringing in her ears.

"W-what just happened?" she asked, hating that her voice shook along with the rest of her.

The man's lips flattened as he shook his head. "They were about to use magic to see if anyone was veiled."

With those words, Breda realized that her first conclusion had been right. She was with two Reapers. If she feared the soldiers, she was absolutely terrified of the Reapers. She looked to her left, then her right, searching for some way to get away.

"There's nowhere you can go," the woman said as she walked up behind Breda.

Breda whirled around so fast, she tripped and twisted her ankle, sending her crashing to her bum.

The woman sighed dramatically. "We just saved your arse. If that doesn't prove we're not with the Others, I'm not sure what will."

"She knows who we are," the man said.

The woman threw up her hands and rolled her eyes. "Brilliant. Exactly what we were trying to prevent. You know what this means, don't you?"

"What did you expect after what just happened?" he asked her.

She pulled a face. "Oh, I don't know. Maybe we should've left her there."

"We hadn't asked her anything yet."

"And look at us now," the woman snapped.

Breda used her magic to heal her sprain as she listened to the two Reapers. Six months ago, she had been like any other Fae, believing that the Reapers were only a myth, stories told to frighten the young into behaving. The Others spoke often and loud to anyone who listened that the Reapers were real. Still, knowing something and coming face-to-face with it were two very different beasts.

The woman put her hands on her hips and turned her back to Breda as she shook her head. The man faced Breda, watching her with his piercing silver eyes.

"You needn't fear us," he told her.

She got to her feet, testing her bad ankle to make sure it was healed. "Hmm. I disagree. You came looking for me. Doesn't that usually mean you've come for my soul?"

"Usually," the woman replied without looking her way.

"We already told you, we just wanted to ask a few questions. The first was if you knew the Others. We now have that answer."

Breda swallowed, trying to moisten her mouth and throat. "You don't know anything."

"Then tell us," he implored.

Tears filled her eyes. She hastily blinked them away. "Those Fae are the worst," she said, barely getting the last word out before her throat closed with emotion.

"We know," the woman said as she faced Breda. "We're fighting them. Not just for ourselves, but for all Fae. And even mortals."

Two tears spilled onto Breda's cheeks. She quickly wiped them away. This was her chance. It was risky, but what choice did she have? "I'll tell you anything you want to know."

"Great," the woman said.

"On one condition," Breda continued.

The man drew in a breath and slowly released it. "What's that?"

Breda looked from one to the other. "That you two vow you won't allow the Others or their soldiers to get me. That you'll do whatever it takes, including taking my life, so I don't fall into their hands."

"Bloody hell," the woman murmured in irritation.

The man stuck out his hand. "Deal."

"Vow it," Breda pressed.

The man didn't hesitate. "I vow to keep you from the Others and their soldiers, even if that means taking your life."

Breda shook his hand then looked at the woman.

She rolled her red eyes and said, "I vow to keep you from the Others and their soldiers, even if it means taking your life."

Breda breathed a sigh of relief.

"I'm Torin," the man said. He motioned to the woman with his thumb. "That's Aisling."

Breda nodded. "I suppose you want to start now?"

"The sooner, the better," Aisling said.

Breda met Torin's gaze. She couldn't tell what he was thinking, but she discovered that she was insanely curious to know. That same curiosity had gotten her into her present predicament. Even knowing that, she couldn't look away. There was something about him, something she couldn't quite put her finger on.

But she knew one thing. She was calmer with him near.

CHAPTER THREE

"I guess you already know my name is Breda."

Torin nodded slowly. The fact that she was more terrified of the Others than she was of the Reapers went a long way in confirming that the Others were moving into dangerous territory.

Breda glanced around before rubbing a hand down her other arm. "I don't like being out in the open like this."

"No one will find you here," Aisling told her.

Breda threw up her hands and turned in a circle. "Really? Because we look pretty damn exposed to me."

"I put a veil around us. No one can see or hear us," Aisling retorted.

Breda frowned, duly chastised. "Oh."

Torin crossed his arms over his chest. "We gave you our vow. That isn't something we take lightly."

"After the things I've seen and heard, you'll have to forgive me if I don't hand you all of my trust at once," Breda said.

Aisling snorted loudly. "I thought we'd been through all of this already."

Torin wouldn't get drawn into another debate when there were things to learn. He caught Breda's gaze. "Were you part of the Others?"

"Define *part*," she said.

Aisling sighed loudly. "If getting answers is going to be like pulling teeth, tell us now, and I'll lower the veil protecting you."

"And you," Breda snapped. Then she took a deep breath and released it. "I'm not trying to be difficult. The answer to Torin's question isn't simple. The Others are a hierarchy. The leaders are the Six, as we call them. Second in line are those waiting their turn to be in the Six. These are the truly devote. Next are the soldiers, who are just as devote, but use their skills and power to ensure the Six continue. Forth are those who recruit Fae to join. It's their job to grow the ranks at any cost. The final two levels are those recruited and learning about the Others, and those who want to join."

Torin's question had been a bit of a test. He'd wanted to know just how deeply Breda had been in the organization. He had his answer. "And which were you?"

Breda looked away, refusing to meet his gaze. "I was recruited. I...I also recruited."

"For how long?" Aisling asked.

Breda swallowed. "Eight months or so."

Torin looked at Aisling to see her worried frown. He then turned his attention back to Breda. "What happened to make you run from them?"

"I learned about the Reapers, or rather, you."

He shouldn't have been shocked to hear Breda say the words, but he was. "How did you learn of us?"

"They hold weekly meetings that everyone must attend without fail. There're no excuses, no reason for missing one. If you do, you're out. And if you're out, they take your life," Breda told them as she looked their way.

Aisling shrugged half-heartedly. "If they want their secrets kept, that's to be expected."

"What happens at the meetings?" Torin asked.

Breda's red eyes met his. "Everyone is present, but only the Six interact. We're there simply to watch and learn. The Six have a private meeting before ours."

"Who are the Six? Do you know their names?" Aisling pressed.

Breda shook her head. "They don't use names. I'm sure they know who each other is, just as they know the rest of us, but we don't know their names."

"What about how many Light and Dark?" Torin asked.

"Three Light. Three Dark. There's a balance. Always," Breda answered.

Aisling's frown deepened. "That sounds very similar to—"

"I know," Torin said before she could finish.

Breda looked from him to Aisling. "You mean Death?"

Shite. How much did the Others know? Torin clenched his teeth, becoming more worried as each tidbit of information was revealed.

"We'll get back to the group in a sec," Aisling said. "Right now, I want to know everything you know about us."

Breda took a half-step back. Anyone in their right mind would have, given the fury rolling off Aisling. Torin couldn't blame Aisling, though. He was upset, as well.

"She isn't upset with you," he told Breda.

Aisling snorted. "On the contrary."

Torin snapped his head to her as he dropped his arms to his sides. "Aisling."

"She's part of them, Torin."

"The fact that they came after her says otherwise."

Aisling's nostrils flared. "It could be a trap for us."

"It isn't," Breda said.

Torin glanced at her. "Why not?"

Breda swallowed loudly as she lifted her chin. "I learned about the Others from listening to the Fae. There was little knowledge of what the group did, but to listen to everyone else who spoke of them with reverence…it was something I wanted to know more about. My curiosity has gotten me into bad situations before. I never thought it would lead to something like this."

"Go on," Aisling urged in a tight voice.

Torin nodded to Breda when the Dark Fae looked at him.

"It didn't take much for me to get recruited. I went to the meetings and was soon taken in. I didn't believe everything I was told. I've heard enough sales pitches in my life to know when someone is trying to deceive me."

Aisling scrunched up her face in shock. "And you still wanted in?"

Breda nodded. "The more I learned, the more curious I became. Sadly, my biggest vice is letting my curiosity dictate my actions. If that many Fae were going to the Others in droves, there had to be a reason."

"You got in. Then what?" Torin asked.

Breda shifted her feet. "I'm not going to lie. I liked hearing how a united, strong Fae was the next step for us. However, if I ever brought up the fact that Fae were attempting that already with the Council, I was quickly shut down. After the second time, one of the soldiers took me aside after a meeting and told me that I was never to speak out like that again. I've run into some nasty beings before, but the soldiers…well, they're different. As you saw at the pub."

"That isn't the first time we've encountered them," Aisling said indifferently.

Torin cleared his throat. "How long were you in the organization before you learned about the Reapers?"

"Maybe a month," Breda said with a shrug. "They brought it up very casually during a meeting. At first, I thought it was a joke. I soon realized the opposite was true."

"What did they say?" Aisling demanded.

Breda licked her lips in a nervous gesture. "They said the Reapers were a scourge for the Fae, and that the Reapers and their leader, Death, were holding the Fae back from their true destiny."

"And?" Torin pushed her to continue.

Breda looked at the ground for a heartbeat. "That Reapers were more powerful than any Fae, and it was because of you that the Fae decided to create the Others."

"They didn't create the first group," Aisling snapped. "The Fae were a part of the first Others, but their goal was to destroy the Dragon Kings. That didn't turn out too well, did it?"

Torin had been watching Breda closely. "What made you decide to leave the Others?"

"I learned what they did to the Fae who weren't accepted into the organization."

"You mean how they kill them and absorb their magic?" Torin asked.

Breda nodded woodenly. "The Six take their magic. That would've been me had I not been accepted."

"We need a description of each of the Six. You said there were equal Light and Dark. What about male and female?" Aisling asked.

Breda answered, "One male, five females."

Torin turned to Aisling. "I'll take this information back to the rest. See if you can get anything else."

"I'll go. I need to cool off," Aisling told him before she teleported out.

Torin swallowed before he turned his head to Breda. "Thank you for sharing all of that. We're going to have more questions."

"I assumed. I'll tell you all that I know."

"You sure you'll share everything?"

She frowned, affronted that he would question her. "Of course."

"I don't think so."

Her fear dissipated as her anger grew. "You know me so well that you can determine when I'm keeping something back?"

"You're hiding something. Of that, I'm positive. I've not figured out what it is yet, but I will. If you're a spy for the Others—"

"I'm not," she snapped.

"If you are, things won't go well for you."

She lifted her chin. "I'm not a spy. I ran from them. You were there."

"I've seen my share of betrayals, Breda. Some of them are so good that others have no idea what's about to happen. You could be a very good actress, for all I know."

She threw up her hands in defeat. "Nothing I say will convince you I'm not a spy."

"Tell me what you're hiding."

She took a step back, wariness clouding her expression.

He held her gaze, refusing to let her get away. "Don't bother trying to teleport. You won't get anywhere. The veil is hiding you from everyone, but it's also keeping you here."

"I didn't try to leave."

That made him frown. The first thing a Fae did in a situation they couldn't win was jump away. Why wasn't Breda? Was she that fearful of the Others and their soldiers that it never crossed her mind?

Or was there another reason she didn't teleport out?

Torin couldn't help but wonder if she was a spy. It would be a tactic he would use if he were able. Put someone amid a bad situation so the enemy took her and attempted to gain her trust. Then she could attack from within. So far, neither he nor Aisling had said anything about the Reapers. Breda hadn't asked, either. That could be because she thought she knew everything already, or she was simply waiting for an opportune time to ask.

"It's better if you tell me what you're hiding now," Torin told her. "Don't make me find out on my own."

Her chin lifted in defiance. "I'm not hiding anything."

With every lie she told, it eroded the fragile trust they had been building. Torin tried another tactic. "Tell me how, why, and when you left the Others."

"I left today. I thought I would have a day or two to figure out my next move."

"You didn't have a plan in place before you left?" That knowledge didn't sit well with him.

She shook her head. "I'd become more and more uneasy with the organization over the past few months. I searched for a way out but couldn't find one. I was putting together an escape plan when someone else tried to leave. The soldiers hunted them down like an animal. They brought the Fae back and tortured her in front of everyone. I couldn't take another minute. I knew it was only a matter of time before they realized that I wasn't fully part of the organization as they wanted. Soon, I'd have to recruit more Fae again. I didn't want to be responsible for any more deaths."

Torin frowned. That admission coming from a Dark Fae was as confusing as a fish that didn't like water. And it confirmed that she was definitely hiding something.

CHAPTER FOUR

Somewhere in Ireland…

"They failed to find Breda."

The other five members looked at her as she returned to the circle. She met each of their gazes, waiting for a response.

It was Dark 1, the only male, who spoke first. "Where did the soldiers lose her?"

"A pub in Dublin called the Sly Stag," she answered.

Light 3 nodded her head. "I know of that establishment. Were the soldiers discreet?"

She shook her head.

Dark 2 twisted her lips, her irritation plain. "That's a pity."

Dark 3 asked, "How did the soldiers lose her? They knew she was there."

"She had help," Light 2 answered before she could.

Dark 1 frowned, his bushy, black and silver brows snapping together. "That can't be."

"It was only a matter of time before the Reapers discovered that we knew of them," Light 2 replied.

Light 3 shrugged. "Maybe it's better the Reapers know."

"We've lost the advantage of a surprise attack," Dark 2 stated.

Dark 3 rolled her eyes. "We lost that when Borgar and Hemming never returned from Dorcha's meetings at Moorehall searching for Reapers. I said then that Reapers killed them. None of you believed me."

She raised her hand to silence them when they spoke at once. "We Six exist because we have solidarity on our side. Tens of thousands of Fae are out there waiting to become one of us. We have hundreds already here, learning what we are. We're altering perceptions and beliefs. It doesn't matter how powerful the Reapers are. They won't be able to stand against what we're building. What we've already built. Nor will they be able to withstand our combined power that grows with every meeting our followers have."

"We've not tested our power against anything more than a few Fae," Dark 1 said.

She smiled, not at all ruffled by the unease moving through the others. "You're worried we won't be able to defeat the Reapers. I know we will. You're worried what will happen when Death comes for us. I'm not. I know nothing in the universe can go up against us. There's a reason the Light and Dark never joined forces. Death is responsible for that. So are the Reapers. They knew if we ever put aside our differences, we would learn what our combined magic could do."

"I, for one, am ready for it," Dark 3 said. "I'm tired of having to do whatever the Dragon Kings say. There are more than enough mortals on this realm to feed every Dark for several years."

Light 2 rolled her eyes. "And once the humans are gone?"

"We fight the Kings and take over, of course," Dark 2 said.

She smiled. "Or we remove the Kings beforehand. The rule of the Light only being able to sleep with a mortal once is absurd. Who cares if they're never able to have a fulfilling relationship with one of their kind after sampling the pleasures of a Fae? It isn't our fault we're beautiful and can give pleasure unlike any other creature. We shouldn't be penalized for what was naturally given to us."

Dark 1 caught her gaze. "All of this is well and good, but that doesn't solve the matter of Breda. If she's with the Reapers, she can tell them our secrets."

"Do you honestly think the Reapers will believe her?" Light 3 asked with a laugh.

She clasped her hands before her. "No one who has tried to leave us has been successful. If Breda believes the Reapers can keep her safe, she's going to learn the hard way how wrong she is. We know magic now that can penetrate through a Reaper's veil to reveal them."

"We don't know how to find them, though," Light 2 said.

She bowed her head in acknowledgement. "Then we work harder to ensure that we can. Until then, the soldiers know to search for Breda and the Reapers. Get the word out to all Fae, give them Breda's description. Someone will see her. Make sure to get let it be known that we're also looking for Breda's accomplices."

"So, we'll get a description of a Reaper or two." Dark 2 grinned. "Brilliant."

Breda held Torin's gaze, fear and panic running through her. He looked as if he could see right through her soul—to her secret.

Her heart thumped wildly, and her palms were damp. But she didn't look away. She couldn't. Her secret was the only thing keeping her alive. She couldn't let it be known. Ever.

Torin sighed. It wasn't a resounding sigh, but a *we'll-return-to-this-later* sound. She wasn't looking forward to that discussion. This one had been difficult enough. Hopefully, she had done enough to make him believe that she wasn't hiding anything. But, on the off chance she hadn't, she needed to think of a way to dissuade him.

If she couldn't, then things would get hairy, really quick.

"Where are the meetings?" Torin asked.

Thankful for a change in the conversation, Breda shook her head. "We arrive at a designated spot, and the soldiers take us. I have no idea of the actual location."

"Did you see anything that you could pick out? Something in the landscape?"

"We were inside a building."

"Could you see outside the windows to anything like water or a port?"

She shook her head again. "There were no windows. The first time I was brought to the meeting, I thought we were underground. The room was dark except for six lights pointed toward a stage in the middle. We were seated in stadium seats that encircled the stage. The Six appeared and stood in the light, facing each other in a circle, talking as if we weren't there."

"That place could be anywhere in the realm," Torin said with a frown.

"Since they went to great lengths to ensure that none of us knew where we were, I think that's the point."

Torin gave her a flat look. "Did you see each of the Six enough to describe them?"

"Absolutely. You think that will be enough?"

He didn't answer, which told her that he wasn't ready to share the goings-on of Reaper life with her. Not that she could blame him. If she weren't running for her life from the soldiers, she wouldn't be telling him the things she was now. She had always been private about her life. It felt odd and intrusive to have someone asking such specific questions.

It took her a moment to realize he hadn't posed another query. That's when she realized that he was staring at her. His intense look made her nervous. On the one hand, he was gorgeous, and his attention was flattering.

On the other, he was only looking because she had something he wanted.

"What?" she finally asked.

Torin twisted his lips. "How many have tried to leave the Others?"

"I don't know. Sometimes, the soldiers bring them back to show what happens to those who betray the organization, but I know that sometimes they don't."

"How do you know?"

Breda shoved her hair to the other side of her head and ran her palm against the shaved sections. "I stood near a woman my first couple of months attending the meetings. We struck up a conversation once. After that, we stood beside each other each time. She was Light Fae, and it was obvious that she had been completely taken in by the Others. She said a few things that made me think she regretted her decision. By that point, I'd realized that if they wanted you to join, you either did it or they killed you. There wasn't a third option. I told her that, but she said she couldn't, in good conscience, remain. The next meeting, she wasn't there. She's never been back."

"How do you know she didn't get away?"

"The soldiers asked me questions about her. It was obvious by the way they worded things that they had already captured her."

Torin's brow furrowed. "Then why not make an example out of her like the rest?"

"I have no idea. But I do know she's dead now—or close to it."

"Knowing all that you did, you still left?"

Breda smiled sadly. "Her words replayed in my head for weeks. There was so much I didn't like about the Others. I wasn't the only one. Many are fanatics and eager to do whatever it takes to become an Other. Like the soldiers. Then there were those who did their best to hide their abhorrence for the atrocities being done."

"You're Dark."

"And because I'm Dark, I shouldn't be repulsed by the murder of others?" she countered in an even tone, belying the ire within.

Torin glanced at the ground. "What I meant was that the Dark don't mind killing or murder."

She touched her black hair laced with silver. "You think this is glamour?"

"I know it isn't."

Breda was curious to know how he knew such a thing, but she didn't ask since she knew he wouldn't disclose such information. "Does it bother you that I'm Dark?"

"Aisling is Dark."

"That didn't answer my question."

"I've learned that not everything is as it seems, and until you live someone else's life, you have no right to judge."

She bowed her head, impressed. "Wise words. If only everyone else in the universe felt such a way."

"That isn't in our nature."

"Sadly, that's true. But you've still not answered my question."

His lips turned up in a quick grin. "I don't know your past. You don't know mine. What you've done to become Dark is your story. We didn't come looking for you because you're Dark. We came looking because of who you are."

She frowned and moved closer to him. "Wait. What? How did you know about me?"

"Why does it matter?"

"Because I told no one I was an Other."

He shot her a dry look. "If you recruited Fae to join, obviously you did."

She drew back, shocked because he was right. "Who told you?"

"We've known about the Others for some time."

"Can you give me a straight answer?" she demanded, her voice rising in her irritation. All she could think about was her family.

He studied her for a moment. "There is a list of names. We've been going down it."

"Would you have saved me had I not had information?" She shook her head, lifting her hand. "Never mind. I don't want to know the answer."

"The answer is yes," Torin replied. "I'm not in the habit of watching anyone get murdered, especially by soldiers of the Others. I've seen their handiwork firsthand."

She fiddled with a chip in her thumbnail. "I'm glad you and Aisling were there when they came. I don't want to think about what might be happening now if you hadn't. So, thank you."

"You're welcome."

"What else do you want to know? I want to make sure I'm giving you whatever you need."

He scratched his temple. "Do you know how the Others found out about the Reapers?"

"One of the Six has seen one of you. They had personal knowledge and visual confirmation of something that occurred a few years ago."

"What was the event?" Torin asked, moving closer.

Breda saw the concern in his silver eyes. "I-I don't remember."

"Think!" he barked.

"I'm trying," she snapped. "I can't do anything with you bellowing at me."

The instant the words were out of her mouth, he blinked and got control of his fury. "Apologies. It's just information I need."

"I understand." And she did. "Let me think on it."

He nodded and raked his hand through his hair as he turned and started to pace. "You said a few years ago?"

"Yes," Breda replied.

"Hm. That could be that one. Or that one. Oh. It might be that one," he said, more to himself than her.

Her curiosity grew to the point she almost asked about each of those, but then she remembered why she was in her present predicament and decided to keep her mouth closed.

She chuckled to herself. "Maybe I am growing up, finally," she murmured.

Or maybe it was just wishful thinking.

CHAPTER FIVE

Torin wished he knew exactly when someone had seen them. The Reapers were careful about making sure no outsiders—especially the Fae—saw them. But that didn't mean someone hadn't somehow slipped through and witnessed something. He racked his brain, trying to think of where it could have been or who he and his fellow Reapers could've battled for a Fae to realize what they were.

No matter how hard he searched, he couldn't come up with a place.

His gaze swung to Breda. "Still nothing?"

"It was a big battle. Something important."

He faced her. "You're sure?"

She parted her lips and then shrugged. "I wasn't focused on where you were seen. I was more interested in the Reapers in general and how the Six knew of you."

"And it was a woman?"

"A Light Fae, yes."

They'd had a few skirmishes at the Light Castle. Specifically, when Talin had been sent in as a spy and met Neve Everwood. Things hadn't gone well for the first group of Reapers. That was before Erith had told them about the second group she had been putting together—Torin's group.

Torin wished he could ask Breda specific questions, but he held back since he was still uncertain if she was a spy. He didn't want to inadvertently tell her something that she didn't already know. But how could he determine where the Reapers had been seen if he didn't get specifics?

Before he could delve deeper, he spotted someone at the edge of the field, far from them. The instant Torin saw the black attire, he knew it was a soldier of the Others. No one should've found them. The fact that a soldier had didn't bode well. Torin debated whether to attack. He wasn't afraid of going up against a soldier. He knew he would emerge victorious. The problem was, more would likely come if the soldier didn't return. Then they would know for certain that Reapers had been there.

Two more soldiers appeared. The veil dome Aisling had erected easily enclosed Breda and him. Torin could broaden it, but he might alert the soldiers. It was better if he did nothing.

"Shite," Breda said as she pointed behind him. "A-a soldier is here."

"How many?"

A small frown creased her face. "One."

"That makes four."

"Four?" she asked in a startled voice and spun around to look behind her.

She stumbled back a few steps at the sight of the soldiers. In two strides, Torin was beside her, steadying her.

"How did they find us?" she asked, her voice rising.

"I don't know."

His instinct was to go after those tracking him and Breda, but he also had a duty to her. She had put her life in his hands. He'd given her a vow, and he didn't make promises lightly. This was the second time he had encountered the soldiers with Breda. Just as before, she shook with terror.

She couldn't fake something like that.

Her panic was real. Her terror palpable. He had no idea what she had seen the soldiers do, but it had left an indelible mark upon her. Torin put his hands on her shoulders. She pressed her back against him and gripped his jeans with her hands.

"Remember," he reminded her. "They can't see or hear us."

"Then how are they here?"

"We don't know what kind of power they or the Six have. It's why Aisling erected the veil. We didn't want anyone stumbling across us."

Breda shook her head. "There's nowhere I can go, is there? They'll hunt me down until they find me."

"You're with me now. No one, not a soldier, not an Other, will get through me to you."

Breda leaned her head back to look up at him. "Even though I'm one of them?"

"You *were* one. You're under the Reapers' protection now."

Relief moved across her face. "Thank you."

Torin didn't like the emotion that went through him at her words. He shoved it aside and lifted his gaze to the soldiers. These Fae were powerful. While the Reapers had gone up against soldiers recently and won, he and his brethren never took anything for granted. They evaluated each adversary individually and adjusted their attack and magic for each.

Breda returned her attention to the soldiers. "What do we do?"

"Nothing," Torin said.

"If backed against a wall, I'll fight. But I'd rather run."

He inwardly smiled at her candid comment. "We do nothing."

"What if they attack?"

"Then *I* do something."

"It might be good if Aisling returns now."

What they needed was his group of Reapers. "Eoghan," he said softly.

Within a heartbeat, the leader of his group appeared before them. Eoghan's quicksilver eyes took in Torin and Breda, then looked around. He blew out a breath as he faced Torin once more. "When did they arrive?"

"A few minutes ago. They've not moved," Torin said.

Eoghan nodded and teleported out once more.

"Where did he go?" Breda asked in a high-pitched voice.

Torin lightly squeezed her shoulders. "He'll be back."

But his words had little effect on her. Suddenly, there was a fifth arrival. Torin's mouth parted in astonishment when he saw Xaneth. The royal Light Fae killed the first soldier before Torin knew what had happened. The others immediately began hurling volleys of iridescent magic balls at Xaneth.

One landed on Xaneth's left shoulder, knocking him back. Xaneth didn't pause as he started toward his next target, the soldier on his right. Torin took a step toward Xaneth, wanting to help the Fae. Breda grabbed Torin's hand and tugged him to a stop.

Torin didn't take his gaze from Xaneth as the Fae walked through the onslaught of orbs descending all around him. Some landed on the ground, sizzling as they melted the grass and dirt to disappear into the earth. Others hit Xaneth time and again. No matter how large the orbs were, they didn't stop him. He kept walking like a man on a mission.

The other two soldiers realized that something was amiss with Xaneth and hurried to help their comrade. But it was too late. Xaneth had already reached him and snapped his neck. The fact that the royal wasn't using magic confused and intrigued Torin.

With more orbs of magic directed at him, Xaneth quickly and effortlessly took out the remaining two soldiers. When they were dead, their bodies disintegrating and turning to ash, Xaneth lifted his head and looked right at Torin. Shocked, Torin could only blink in response.

"I didn't think anyone could see us," Breda said in a soft whisper.

"They're not supposed to."

She made a sound at the back of her throat. "Um…I hate to break it to you, but he sure does."

Torin gently pulled his hand from Breda and started toward Xaneth. He only took two steps before the royal Fae vanished. Torin stared at the spot where Xaneth had been. They had looked for him for months. They'd gotten close recently, but he'd disappeared before anyone could talk to him. Just as he had done this time. Xaneth had told them to forget him, but the Reapers owed him. And they wanted to pay up.

"Where are the fekkers?" Aisling asked from behind him.

Eoghan grunted. "They were here. Torin? Did they leave?"

"A Light with a death wish killed them," Breda replied.

Torin turned to see the others of his unit of Reapers. His gaze moved between Bradach, Dubhan, Cathal, Rordan, Eoghan, and Balladyn, ending at Aisling.

"What?" Aisling asked with a frown. Then her brow smoothed out. "He was here?"

Torin nodded. "Just now."

Before anyone could stop her, Aisling jumped to the other side of the protective veil.

"How did we miss him again?" Dubhan asked incredulously.

It was Balladyn who said, "Because he doesn't want to be found."

"How did he find Torin?" Bradach asked.

Rordan shook his head. "We still don't know how he found us last time."

"You all know what to do," Eoghan said. "I have to take this news back."

Torin blew out a breath and scrubbed a hand down his face as Balladyn jumped to Aisling to help her search for clues to where Xaneth might have gone. Then Torin's gaze landed on Breda. He'd forgotten about her.

"It's okay," she said with a flippant shrug.

He frowned. "What is?"

"That you forgot I was here."

Duly chastised, he grimaced. "The Fae that was here is a friend who was tortured awhile ago. He helped us, and now we want to help him."

"He doesn't seem to want or need your aid," Breda stated the obvious.

Torin couldn't disagree with her.

"More soldiers will come," Rordan said.

Bradach smiled. "I'm ready and eager."

"Just like last time," Dubhan said with a nod.

Torin watched Breda observe each Reaper, taking everything in. She was quiet, making it easy to overlook her. His brow furrowed when he realized that while she wasn't petite in stature, it was almost as if she disappeared from thought if someone weren't looking at her. He'd seen all kinds of Fae magic, but he'd never witnessed anything like this before. It was almost as if she wanted to be unnoticed. She got quiet, almost folded into herself so as not to draw attention. That went against what Fae normally did.

"We found nothing," Balladyn said as he and Aisling returned.

Torin glanced at Aisling, but her gaze was on the ground. If there was any doubt that she felt something for Xaneth, each time they came close to finding the royal Fae, the reservations eroded.

"Don't," she said when Cathal touched her arm.

Torin caught Balladyn's gaze. The ex-King of the Dark shook his head, confirming there wasn't anything to find. Xaneth was learning to cover his tracks well. But they were Reapers. Eventually, they would find him. Torin wasn't sure if that would be good or not. Aisling was family, and none of them wanted to see her hurt. Unfortunately, it didn't look like it could go any other way.

"The fact that the soldiers found you means they're either tracking us," Dubhan said, then moved his gaze to Breda. "Or her."

Bradach crossed his arms over his chest. "There's one place we can go where they can't follow."

"No," Torin said, knowing Bradach was referring to Death's realm, their home. "I don't want to test the Six and see how far their reach extends."

Balladyn shrugged, a grin tugging at the corners of his lips. "There's another place."

"I like it," Rordan said with a smile.

Dubhan laughed, nodding.

Torin slid his gaze to Aisling. She gave him a slight dip of her chin. "It's perfect."

Just as he was about to call for Eoghan, their leader returned.

Eoghan looked around the group, letting his gaze rest on Breda for a heartbeat. "We won't attempt to track Xaneth," he began.

"I can go on my own," Aisling stated.

Eoghan's gaze moved to her. "You're needed with your team. We've not forgotten Xaneth, but we need to put an end to the Others first."

"Look at what he did," she said as she motioned to the ash of the dead soldiers. "We need him."

Cathal's lips twisted. "She's not wrong."

"We have our orders," Eoghan replied.

Torin asked, "What are those?"

"Keep Breda alive as we get more details from her about the Others," Eoghan explained.

Balladyn shook his head. "She can't remain on this realm. Not after how easily the soldiers found her."

"I agree," Eoghan said. He looked at each of them. "There is a realm none would think to go to."

Torin grinned. "We were thinking the same thing."

Eoghan looked at Torin and then Aisling. "You two take Breda. We'll be along shortly."

CHAPTER SIX

It was unnerving to be around so many Reapers. Breda tried to remember faces and attributes, but she knew she wouldn't be able to. She only heard two other names: Xaneth and Eoghan. Her curiosity about Xaneth nearly got the better of her. She had so many questions. The first was why the Reapers were so intent on finding him.

And why Xaneth wanted nothing to do with them.

The look on Aisling's face stopped Breda short of asking any questions. Maybe if she were alone with Torin, she might pose some queries. Though she wouldn't be so cruel as to ask Aisling. And that had nothing to do with how the rest of the Reapers watched Aisling so protectively—though it helped.

Breda had never had anyone look at her the way the Reapers did Aisling. She envied the female Reaper. She was clearly loved and protected. Breda wondered if Aisling had any idea how much the others cared about her.

A million other questions swarmed Breda's mind. Like where in the bloody hell was this other realm the Reapers were taking her? When she turned to Torin to ask, he shook his head at her before looking away. She was miffed at being silenced, but at the moment, she didn't want the others to notice her. It was interesting being able to observe the Reapers. She doubted many had been in her situation and got to see this elite unit function in such a way.

Before she knew it, Eoghan gave his final order. She barely registered it before Torin grabbed her, and she found herself in front of a Fae doorway. Breda tried to back up, not wanting to go anywhere until she found out where it was.

"Wait," she said.

Torin didn't loosen his hold. "There's no time."

"I just—"

"Now," Aisling spoke over her and gave her a push from behind as Torin started through the doorway.

In the next instant, Breda found herself standing in a desolate world. "Um…I think there's been a mistake."

"No mistake," Aisling said as she walked past.

Torin released her. "I'm asking you to trust us."

Breda stared into his silver eyes. Everything she'd learned in her life told her not to put her faith in him. But a tiny part of her, the bit she had buried when she was a small child, urged her to trust Torin.

"I gave you my vow," he reminded her.

Breda glanced at Aisling to see that she had paused to look back at them. Finally, Breda nodded at Torin, and they started walking to catch up with Aisling. They seemed to walk for an eternity, but it didn't matter how far they went, everything was still dead.

"It's going to be fine. Just walk through it," Torin suddenly said.

Breda frowned as she jerked her head to him. "Walk through what?"

No sooner had she asked the question than she felt the vibrations growing before her. She couldn't see anything, but she could feel it. Aisling didn't stop walking. Suddenly, she disappeared from view. Breda thought she had teleported away until Torin halted and gave her a nod.

Breda hoped that nod of encouragement wasn't supposed to mean that she should continue toward the vibrations. Unfortunately, she realized that's exactly what it meant. Breda drew in a deep breath and started forward. She felt something warm and fuzzy wash over her, almost like static electricity. Her breath left her in a whoosh when she gazed upon the verdant, lush land around her.

"Where are we?" she asked.

Aisling knelt beside a cluster of small, white flowers and leaned down to smell them. "The Fae Realm."

"But...I thought it had been destroyed."

Torin came up beside her. "It was. Rhi began healing it."

"Rhi?" Breda asked in surprise. "The same Rhi who is mated to Constantine, King of Dragon Kings? The same Rhi who helped to take out Usaeil, Queen of the Light?"

Aisling got to her feet. "Usaeil was Rhi's mother."

"Bloody hell," Breda mumbled in shock.

Torin drew in a breath and slowly released it as he closed his eyes. "A lot has happened among the Fae that few know about."

"Like the healing of the realm. Why hasn't anyone said anything?" Breda asked.

Torin turned his head to look at her. "Rhi told them. I don't know if they believed her since I've not seen any. What do you think will happen?"

Breda looked around at the beauty that defied words. The birdsong was loud and joyful. The sun shone bright and warm, the breeze was cool. It was a perfect world, unmarred by war or greed —the very things that had ripped it apart to begin with. She had never thought to look upon the Fae Realm, and yet, here she was.

"The Fae will flock here," she said in answer. "Some will try to keep the beauty, but others won't care. The cycle that destroyed the realm and the Fae will begin again. I doubt that the Council of Fae would continue. The Dark would find another monarch, as would the Light."

She blinked to find both Aisling and Torin staring at her with weird expressions on their faces. "What?" she asked. "This is a treasure. No one should know of this. Not even me. Rhi made a mistake mentioning it."

"It will stay secret if the doorways are removed," Aisling said.

Torin shot her a concerned look before he told Breda, "The realm is still healing. Even when it's fully healed I, too, think it should remain untouched."

"It won't happen. Fae come here all the time. There are those who can't let go of the past, and those who will want to see if what Rhi said is true. Younger Fae hear the stories of this realm and want a chance to see it for themselves," she said.

Aisling cocked her head to the side. "How many times have you been here?"

"This is my first time." Breda hoped that by answering truthfully, she hadn't revealed anything telling about herself.

Torin started walking, and she and Aisling fell into step alongside him. He glanced at Breda. "We walked a considerable way to get here. I'm not sure many would venture too deeply into the realm."

"They might if they learn that Rhi is healing it," Aisling added.

Breda shrugged. "Maybe it's because I've been around the worst of the Fae for so long, but I can see this being discovered sooner rather than later."

"For now, it's a safe place for you to hide from the Others," Torin said.

Aisling lengthened her stride and walked ahead of them. She hadn't been the same since Xaneth had appeared. Breda barely knew Aisling. Even if they had been close, Breda still wouldn't know how to ask if she was all right.

"You're worried about her?" Torin asked.

Breda glanced at him. "I hear surprise in your voice."

"I am," he admitted.

She shrugged, wrinkling her nose. "I think it's because of the look on her face when she knew Xaneth was there. Are they together?"

"Like a couple? No. At least, not that I'm aware."

"She acted like it."

His gaze slid to Aisling. "That she does."

"You and the others care deeply about her."

"We care deeply about each other. We're family."

Breda had sensed that. She had thought she'd found a family with the Others. How wrong she had been. "That must be nice."

"More than you realize."

That got her attention. "Meaning?"

Torin held her gaze for a moment before he sighed. "How do you think Reapers come to be?"

"It's probably like any secret organization. You have to know the right person to get an invite."

"It's not like any organization, secret or otherwise. There are only three criteria that Death considers before an offer is made."

Breda's curiosity exploded. "Like what?"

"Each Reaper is an exceptional fighter."

Well, that automatically excluded her. So much for finding another home. She felt deflated but was still interested in the rest. "And?"

"We were all betrayed."

She was so surprised, she tripped. "What?"

Torin halted a step and a half in front of her and turned to her. "And we were each murdered."

"Bloody hell," she murmured as she let that sink in. Then she studied Torin. "So, you were betrayed and killed?"

He gave a single nod.

"I'm sorry. Did you get revenge on whoever did that to you?"

His chest expanded with his breath. "When we accept Death's offer to become a Reaper, we leave the world and the people we knew behind. Everyone believes we died."

"That way, no one would know what you had become and use it against you," she surmised.

"Precisely."

Then a thought occurred to Breda. "Why are you telling me all of this? Is it because you're going to kill me once I've told you everything about the Others?"

"I don't know what Death has in store, but I can tell you that we don't murder people simply because they don't do what we want."

"But no one is supposed to know who you are. I've seen eight of you now. I might not know names, but if the Others are willing to hunt me down for having information, what's to stop you from doing the same?"

He held her gaze and calmly said, "Nothing."

She had spent her entire life trying to fit in, searching for some kind of family or group where she could be a part of something. Now, it appeared as if she might not ever find that. Not that she blamed the Reapers. Their entire way of life was being threatened.

"Nothing the Reapers are doing has kept the Fae from reaching their full potential," Torin said, breaking into her thoughts. "Death keeps the balance in the Fae. If we were as terrible as the Others make us out to be, we would've taken out Usaeil before she could've done the damage she did. Same with any Dark King who took that throne."

"You were betrayed and killed by Fae. How can you be so forgiving now?"

He shrugged. "I pledged my loyalty to Death."

"And Death is?" Breda asked with raised brows.

Torin glanced away for a heartbeat. "Not someone you want as an enemy. Death is more powerful than any group of Others."

"Could Death have stopped the original Others after the Dragon Kings?"

"Absolutely."

"But she didn't. Why?"

"Death takes her duties as judge and jury seriously. She weighs everything. It would've been simple to step in and take care of everything, but there are lives and destinies at stake."

Breda couldn't imagine having that kind of responsibility. Yet, as she listened to Torin, she heard his respect and admiration. "You like her."

"She's a force, but I do. She's smart and unimaginably powerful."

"Will I get to meet her?"

Torin shrugged. "Maybe."

Breda bit her lip. "Do I want to?"

Torin laughed. "Most probably wouldn't."

Not even that changed her mind about wanting to encounter Death.

CHAPTER SEVEN

They might be on another realm, but that didn't mean Torin let his guard down. It would be easy to relax. After all, it would take some special skills for anyone, much less the Fae Others, to determine where Breda was now. But no one, least of all Torin, would underestimate this powerful new group.

Although, he was beginning to think that it wasn't quite as new as he'd first thought.

Dubhan and his mate, Kyra, were the first to encounter the soldiers. It was because of Kyra's help in searching for Xaneth that they'd stumbled upon a human dwelling with a symbol that Dubhan recognized, since it matched one carved on his childhood home. It turned out to be a symbol of the Others. That'd led them to an old friend of Kyra's. Which, unfortunately, meant his death. Dubhan and Kyra narrowly escaped the soldiers working for the Others.

Then there was Cathal, Sorcha, and Aisling's run-in with them after a bounty had been put on Sorcha's head by a scorned woman out for revenge. Sorcha wasn't just any Druid, she was a Skye Druid, one of the most powerful Druids of them all. She also happened to be a Halfling thanks to her Light Fae father. The magic she possessed was unlike any the Reapers or Death had ever seen. It was formidable and potent—as the soldiers discovered when they tried to attack Cathal and Aisling. If it hadn't been for Sorcha's magic, Torin's two friends would be dead.

That brought him to Rordan, who had gone undercover to see how the Fae were being recruited into the Others. Fianna's brother and father were high in the organization, which gave her access to information. Unfortunately, that brought Rordan face-to-face with two soldiers. However, the Reapers learned that the Others weren't just looking for Reapers. They had a plan to take them out altogether.

Torin glanced at Breda as she walked beside him. She had been looking around the Fae Realm in wonder. He was glad that she was silent because he needed some time with his thoughts. They were too jumbled with everything that had been happening over the last year. Between the Dragon Kings, Fae, and the Druids, there had been some kind of event that needed attention—few of them good.

The Dragon Kings had things under control, at least. It was the Fae and Druids—specifically the Skye Druids—who were looking into creating separate groups of Others that concerned Torin. While the Fae were the only ones that Death was concerned with, Torin didn't want to discount the Druids. They might not have the magic the Dragon Kings or Fae had, but they could be just as dangerous.

His gaze drifted to Breda once more. The pleasure she got from looking at the Fae Realm shocked him. The Dark might appreciate beauty, but few did it with such open admiration as Breda did. Then there was her abhorrence to killing.

Every Fae was born as a Light. It was the seductive power of the Dark that lured them. In order to become Dark, a Fae had to kill. That first life taken took away their silver eyes and made them red. Every death after turned their black hair silver. The more silver in a Dark's hair, the more lives they had taken, be they human or Fae.

The Dark had a particular palate for mortals. The Light did, as well, but they controlled themselves better. The humans were drawn to Fae against their wills. They would ignore everything and everyone just to get a Fae's attention. If that Fae happened to be Light, the mortal might have a single night of unimaginable pleasure. That one night would leave a mark, however. They would never find fulfillment of release in the arms of their kind again. Though, the humans were left with their lives.

Not so with a Dark. They would set up areas that lured mortals to them. The humans would then be caged like animals, waiting for a Dark to choose them. The entire time, the mortals had no concept of the fact that they were being kept as prisoners—and food. When they got picked, the Fae pleasured them for hours, and they became so consumed by bliss that they were totally unaware that their souls were being drained by the Fae having sex with them.

Torin often thought the Dark's way was kinder. The mortal died with pleasure. It was a ghastly way to go, but they didn't know it. Whereas the humans who had an encounter with a Light were left yearning and pining for a being they could never have.

The codependent relationship between the Fae and humans had resulted in many Halflings. Many of the mortals had no idea they had Fae blood running through them. There was a handful who knew—and used it to their advantage, whether in the film industry, modeling, or the like.

The more he looked at Breda, and the more time he spent with her, the more of an enigma she became. The fact that she was hiding something compounded the issue. Despite that, Torin didn't think she was dangerous. At least, not to the Reapers.

She happened to glance his way, their gazes meeting. He frowned as she quickly looked away as if she hadn't wanted to get caught looking at him. He was about to ask her why when it struck him. They had barged in on her, threatened her, saved her from the soldiers, only to take her somewhere she didn't know, trap her, and threaten her again.

No wonder she was so ill at ease with him.

"If we wanted to hurt you, we would've done it already," he told her.

She kept her gaze straight ahead. "If you say so."

"I gave you a vow."

"To keep me from falling into the Others' hands."

He paused, mulling over her words. "You fear me."

She shrugged and snapped off the end of a tall wildflower, sniffing the yellow bud.

"I won't harm you."

"You'll do what you have to do for your family," she replied. There was no heat in her words. It was said as if she were talking about the weather.

Torin glanced at the sky with its slowly moving, thick, white clouds. "What of your family?"

"I don't have one."

"Everyone has family of some kind."

Her derisive snort said otherwise.

Torin tried again. "We might not like our families, but we have them."

"Ask me what you want to know about the Others. I'll answer those questions. I won't respond to anything about my family."

He couldn't argue with that. "Fair enough."

"How much farther are we going?"

"As far as you want."

Her gaze jerked to him in surprise. She studied him a moment as they walked. "Are you serious?"

"Why wouldn't I be?"

"Why would you allow me to make that decision?"

He shrugged. "I felt like it."

She narrowed her eyes on him, then nodded. "Okay. I want to go up there."

He followed her finger to the distant mountains. "How far up?"

"The very top."

"All right."

She glanced away but wore a frown as she returned her gaze to him. "Really?"

"Really," he said with a laugh. He held out his arm. "You can teleport as long as you bring me with you."

Instead of taking him up on the offer, she moved away from him as if the thought of touching him was repulsive. "I was just testing you. I don't care where we go."

It was a lie. Torin knew it. She knew it. But neither said anything. He couldn't help but think it was a good thing that Aisling was behind them. If she had overheard any of that, there was no telling what she would have said. Aisling had always said what was on her mind, but she was more troubled than before.

Torin strode through a meadow to the sound of water trickling over stone. A grove of trees that offered shade was nearby. "How does that look?"

"Beautiful," Breda said with a smile.

He found his lips curving at her response. He lengthened his strides when she quickened her pace. The pure delight on her face was shocking. Either she didn't know that her emotions were so visible, or she didn't care. Either way, Torin enjoyed watching her.

Breda walked to the slow-moving river. In a blink, her boots were gone, and her tight jeans were somehow shoved up to her knees. He watched as she carefully walked into the water. Torin glanced over his shoulder to find Aisling. He lifted his hand to let her know that they had stopped. She returned the gesture, though she slowed her pace. He would leave her be for the moment.

Torin walked to the trees and sat beneath one to watch Breda. She kept close to the shore and walked back and forth in the water. Occasionally, she lifted her face to the sun and took in some deep breaths, all with a wide smile on her face. As a Fae, she would've been able to discover such places on Earth, but she acted as if she had never experienced anything like this before.

The conundrum of Breda grew.

Torin had always been fond of puzzles, but he wondered if he should delve into this one. Much about her concerned him. He didn't deem her dangerous, but he wouldn't underestimate her either. Not with the secrets she had. That was part of what intrigued him about her. He expected her to act one way, and she acted completely different. She wasn't a typical Dark.

Then he recalled when he had first seen her. There had been something different about her. He saw it again, though he couldn't put his finger on exactly what it was. If he wasn't able to see glamour, he would think it was that.

As if she knew that he was staring, she looked at him. Instantly, her smile vanished. It was like she'd put up an invisible wall, hiding from him.

"It's rude to stare," she said as she turned her back to him.

He grinned at having been called out. "Your joy was contagious. I was thinking I hadn't seen anyone look that happy in a long time."

"Oh," she murmured.

Torin wished he could see her face. She was terrible at hiding her emotions, which was probably why she kept her back to him. "There's a lake if you want to go swimming."

"It's okay."

"It's a beautiful area." He got to his feet and walked toward her, stopping a few feet away. "It isn't that far. The walk is stunning, too."

She shook her head. "I don't need to see it."

"I could go for a swim. It might help you relax."

Suddenly, she spun around in a huff. "Can't you take a hint?" she snapped.

Torin was shocked at her anger. "It's just a swim."

"I can't swim. There. I said it. Are you happy?"

He watched her storm off to the grove of trees, wondering what the hell had just happened. As a Fae, all she had to do was use magic if she started to drown. He didn't think there was a Fae who didn't know how to swim. It just proved once again that Breda was full of mysteries.

Torin walked to her as she yanked down the legs of her jeans and put on her boots. She didn't look up at him as he said, "I'm sorry. I didn't realize."

"It's fine."

He squatted in front of her, squinting against the brightness of the sun. "Obviously, it isn't. Someone in the past made you feel inferior for it. There's nothing to be ashamed of."

"Don't be nice. I can't handle nice," she said in a soft voice as she turned her face away.

Everyone had a story. But he had a feeling that Breda's would be difficult to hear. Despite that, he wanted to know about her life and who had treated her so harshly that someone being kind to her was so unfamiliar and caused her to be wary.

Maybe it was because he knew all too well about being made to feel helpless.

CHAPTER EIGHT

Aisling watched Torin and Breda. They were too caught up in whatever they were discussing to notice her. They wouldn't miss her when she left. She took a step back, then another, waiting to see if Torin would look her way.

She was about to teleport to the doorway when a deep voice behind her said, "I didn't figure you were stupid."

Aisling spun around to find Balladyn sitting in the tall grass of the meadow, using his hand to prop himself up as he leaned to the side. One foot was planted, his knee bent while he rested his other arm on it, twirling a blade of grass between his thumb and middle finger. His eyes were closed, and his face was lifted to the sun. His long, black and silver hair was pulled back in a queue. He wore a V-neck black tee with faded denim jeans.

To an onlooker, Balladyn might appear as if he didn't have a care in the world. The truth was that he had been betrayed and murdered by none other than Usaeil, the former Queen of the Light. He'd been one of the Light's best warriors, but Usaeil had taken all that away from him when she had the King of the Dark, Taraeth, capture Balladyn and torture him with the Chains of Mordare until he turned Dark.

The chains were legendary for being unbreakable. Once someone locked them onto a Fae, they couldn't be removed except by the one who secured them. Balladyn had spent decades being tortured. No one, no matter how bright the light was inside them, could withstand such darkness for long. Balladyn had lasted longer than anyone else, but even the great Light warrior had a breaking point.

When he turned Dark, he had fully embraced his new life. He worked his way up to become Taraeth's right hand until he took Taraeth's life to become King of the Dark. Aisling hadn't been surprised at how well Balladyn had fit into the role of King. He had begun work to unite the different factions of Dark into one cohesive unit—and had been making actual progress.

The Dark respected him—a first for a King of the Dark. So, when Usaeil took his life, the Dark joined with the Light to take her down. The strong ground Balladyn had begun to build with the Dark dissolved instantly upon his death.

Even now, while some attempted to form a Fae Council, there were those among the Dark who made plans to take the throne. Aisling wondered what great things Balladyn would've accomplished had he not been murdered.

His head lowered, and his lids lifted so his crimson eyes locked on her. There was no judgment or irritation on his face.

However, she had a healthy dose of both boiling within her. "What are you doing here?"

"We got ahold of an important package that needs to be guarded."

"And no one believed Torin and I could handle that?" she snapped.

Balladyn didn't take the bait and release his fury. "If you think none of us noted your reaction about Xaneth, you're wrong. And need I remind you that you were about to leave?"

"I won't be gone long."

"You know the consequences of disobeying Death."

Aisling flipped her braids over her shoulder. "This was Eoghan's directive, not hers."

"You're intentionally being obtuse. You know that as leader, Eoghan's orders are Death's." Balladyn climbed to his feet with the grace of a feline. "You want to jeopardize everything to find someone who doesn't want to be found?"

"Yes," she replied.

He was silent for a full minute. "Why?"

"That doesn't matter."

"It does," he pressed.

She glared at him. "It doesn't."

"Say it," Balladyn demanded.

Aisling fisted her hands. "Ugh! Because I have to."

"Why?"

She stalked away, trying to get control of the fury roiling violently inside her. She pivoted and returned to Balladyn. "Because I feel it here," she said and touched her chest.

He nodded slowly. "I know."

"Then why did you want me to say it?" she demanded angrily.

"Because you hadn't admitted it to yourself."

She looked away when emotion began choking her.

"I won't stop you," Balladyn said. "I don't think you should go, but I can't make that decision for you."

Aisling swallowed twice before she found her voice. "No one is looking for him."

"We've not given up."

Her gaze slid to Balladyn. "If we wait, it might be too late."

"What do you think will happen to him?"

"I don't know. I don't want to think of it. He's killing. You know what that means."

Sadness filled Balladyn's eyes. "Yes. But I don't believe it's something he would've done on his own. This has to do with Usaeil torturing him all that time."

"He's broken."

"We're all broken. Some more than others."

She blinked rapidly when her eyes stung with unshed tears. "He doesn't deserve to be what he is."

"That's out of our control. Xaneth moved well in both the Light and Dark worlds. We may not know what's driving him now, but he's helping us regardless. Whether he's doing it purposefully or not, I don't know."

Aisling shook her head, frustration burning inside her. "I have to find him."

"I know."

"Don't jeopardize your standing. Take this second chance and live to the fullest."

"I could say the same to you."

She smiled as more tears threatened. "I'm too broken."

"I disagree."

"You were a great King. You'll be an even better Reaper."

He reached over and briefly took her hand, squeezing it. "Take care of yourself."

Aisling glanced over at Torin and Breda once more before jumping to the doorway that led back to Earth.

Balladyn sighed. He walked out of sight of Torin and Breda, annoyed at himself for not being able to convince Aisling to remain.

"You did the best you could," Death said as she materialized before him.

He looked into her lavender eyes. She had an ethereal beauty that defied words. It was Erith who had sent him here. Somehow, she had known exactly what was on Aisling's mind. "What are you going to do?"

"Don't worry about Aisling."

"You could've stopped her from leaving."

Erith lifted her slim black brows and shrugged. "I could have."

"Why didn't you?"

"I've seen the same things you and the other Reapers have," she explained. "I've seen more, actually. Don't think I'm unaware of Aisling's connection to Xaneth. I saw it manifest long before anyone else did."

Balladyn shook his head. "Aisling is one of the best warriors I've ever seen. We need her."

"Why do you think I wanted her as a Reaper? I know how skilled she is."

"Then don't let her go against you so you have to retaliate."

Death tilted her head to the side, her long, blue-black tresses falling over one shoulder. "What do you think I'm going to do?"

"You have few rules, but they're important ones. Obeying you without question is the first."

"So it is."

He squeezed the bridge of his nose with his thumb and forefinger. "I know I'm the newest Reaper, and I'm still learning my way, but don't do this."

"I let Aisling go for the same reason I didn't reap Usaeil's soul before the big battle. Some things are meant to be. I can't step in and fix or stop things simply because I think they're wrong or I don't want someone to get hurt."

Balladyn quirked a brow. "You kept us from dying. That's you stepping in pretty aggressively."

"You weren't a Reaper when we were battling Bran. He betrayed me and the other Reapers in an unforgivable way. And I didn't take his life. I put him on another realm as his prison."

"One he escaped only to go after you and the Reapers. Like any good warrior, you've learned from your leniency."

"And you believe I won't show mercy again? Your first mistake was assuming that prison world was a mercy. Trust me. It wasn't."

Balladyn waved away her words. "Aisling is following her heart. She knows, deep down, that she needs to be there for Xaneth."

"I give you my word that I won't take her life. Is that what you want to hear?"

"It helps, aye."

She studied him before releasing a long breath. "Aisling was right, you know. You're going to make an even better Reaper."

"If I was as good as both of you say, I would've gone with her to watch her back."

"You didn't because you know she wouldn't have allowed it. And neither would I. Aisling has to do this."

Balladyn frowned at her choice of words. "Do you see things about our lives in advance?"

"I'm not all-knowing, if that's what you're asking," she replied with a grin.

"You knew Rhi had to face Usaeil. You knew Aisling has to go after Xaneth."

"And I knew you were going to be King of the Dark."

He snorted. "You really want me to believe you aren't all-knowing?"

"I'm not. Not in the way you think. Sometimes, there's a deep, knowing certainty about things that I can't ignore. The times I have changed things—or attempted to change them—the outcome has been disastrous. You trusted me when you became a Reaper. I'm asking that you continue to trust me. All of you are my family, and I will always protect my family."

Balladyn bowed his head. "I do trust you."

"Stay here with Torin and Breda," she said with a smile before vanishing.

No matter how quickly he killed evil, he caught the stench of it again. It was everywhere, drenching every crack and crevice, every soul. There was no balance of good and evil as he'd been taught. Malevolence ruled.

The proof was all around.

Xaneth gripped his head as pain sliced through it. He clenched his teeth, doing his best not to cry out from the throbbing agony. It was always the same. No matter how much malice he removed, there seemed to be a never-ending pit of it. Once he eradicated it, he would try to rest. Only to be taken down by the excruciating pain.

He wasn't sure how much longer he could keep on this mission. He was physically weary. Emotionally depleted.

Mentally shattered.

Then again, he wasn't sure he could quit, either. Something drove him. He needed to find out what. The only time he slept was when the aching in his head became too much, and he passed out. But it wasn't a restful slumber. His sleep was filled with horrors of his torture at his aunt's hand. It was a good thing that Usaeil was already deceased. Otherwise, he would've sought her out and ripped her limb from limb for what she had done to him—not to mention murdering the rest of their family.

Xaneth felt the darkness at the edges of his vision. When the blessed sleep came for him, his body went slack. He crumpled to the dirty floor of the vacant warehouse in Dublin. Just before the dreamless sleep took over, an image of a beautiful Dark with crimson eyes and black and silver braids flashed in his mind.

She was always there, just out of reach.

And that's where she needed to stay.

"Aisling," he murmured.

CHAPTER NINE

Breda couldn't believe she had told Torin not to be nice. What was wrong with her? She dropped her head back against the tree and closed her eyes, hoping he'd forget that she was there and leave her alone.

The minutes ticked by without a response from him. Breda cracked an eyelid to see what he was doing and discovered that he was gone. Her eyes snapped open to make sure. She found him standing by the river with his back to her and his thumbs hooked in the front pockets of his jeans. At least, he was giving her some space.

She returned to her position as her eyelids drooped. Her body felt so heavy that she couldn't have lifted a finger had she wanted to. It had been days since she had gotten more than cat naps, and her body had been pushed beyond its endurance. She needed sleep. But did she dare let her guard down around the Reapers?

The choice was out of her hands as sleep claimed her in the next breath.

When she opened her eyes, she was on her side on the ground, using her arm as a pillow. She didn't recall moving. She also didn't remember falling asleep. Vibrant purple and pink streaked the sky.

She must have slept for hours. She had to admit, she felt much better.

She pushed herself into a sitting position, yawning. Breda stretched her arms overhead, arching her back and moving her head side to side to stretch out the kinks. On her second yawn, her gaze moved around the area, searching for Torin. She smoothed her hair out of her eyes and tucked the strands behind her ears as she got to her knees and dusted herself off. As she turned to look behind her, she saw a foot dangling in midair. She followed it up to the limb on the next tree, where another Reaper reclined upon the thick branch with his back against the trunk.

His eyes were closed, but she wasn't fooled. No doubt he pretended to sleep. Where was Torin? She turned in a circle, her gaze scanning for any sign of him. The fact that neither he nor Aisling was around worried her. Everyone left her, though, so she shouldn't be surprised.

"He'll be back," the Reaper said.

Breda jerked her head to him, but his eyes were still closed. She wished she had something pithy to say, but she didn't. Instead, she walked to the river and knelt beside it to splash water on her face. It was cool and refreshing. Her eyes no longer felt like sandpaper, but she was still tired. She was beginning to wonder if she would ever feel rested again.

She sat back on her butt and brought her knees up to her chest as she locked her arms around her legs. Her gaze was drawn to the spectacular sunset, but her mind was on the Others. There was no getting around that she was the reason she had the problems she did. Her damn curiosity always got her.

Breda released her hands and got to her feet. She wasn't going to sit around and feel sorry for herself. She'd done enough of that already. She gathered her hair and wound it into a bun on top of her head before stalking back to the trees to search out the other Reaper. Except he was gone.

It was hard not to get irritated. She blew out a breath but kept her sarcastic comment to herself. There was no way they would leave her. Not when she had just begun to give them information.

Breda wasn't a fool. Aisling and Torin had given her their vow, but none of the other Reapers had.

Even if the rest of the Reapers made sure she was kept from the Others, once she had imparted all the information she knew, there would be no need for her. Would they reap her soul? Would they drop her somewhere on Earth so the Others could find her again?

Whatever they did, it would benefit them, not her. But she was used to such events. She had come out on top from the previous ones. She'd find a way to do the same this time.

Hunger pulled her out of her thoughts. She used magic for her favorite meal—tacos. After she'd eaten four in record time, she swallowed the last bite and spotted the Reaper from the tree at the river. Breda held out her hand as her magic formed a margarita on the rocks, heavy on the salt. She licked the salt and drank deeply before standing and walking to the river.

"I'm ready for more questions," she told him.

He glanced at her, his deep red eyes crinkling slightly at the corners. "Are you, now?"

"That's why I'm here. I suppose you're taking over for Torin?"

"Is that what you think?"

She quirked a brow and took another drink. "I've found that when someone answers a question with a question, it's because they have something to hide."

His lips split into a smile. "I like you. You've got spunk. You'll go far."

"Eh," she said with a twist of her lips. "I beg to differ."

"Trust me. I've seen it all. I know what works and what doesn't."

She stared into his eyes and saw truth there. His smile was gone. There was a deep sadness about him. She instantly brought up a shield against it. It had been a long time since her defenses had slipped.

His brow furrowed as he faced her. "What is it? Are you hurt?"

"No," Breda said and took a step back, not that it would do any good since she had already felt the emotions. She used magic to get rid of the margarita, no longer wanting it. "I-I'm fine."

"The hell you are. Tell me what just happened?"

She shook her head, determination filling her as she met his gaze. She pushed aside the residual effects of the sadness and squared her shoulders. "See? I'm fine."

His dubious look told her that he wasn't buying it. "Everyone has secrets. Some are darker than others. If you want to keep yours, then you need to learn to hide things better."

She usually did a much better job. Running from the soldiers and encountering the Reapers had rattled her. "Can we get on with things?"

"Talk all you want," the Reaper said and turned his attention back to the river.

Breda stood there, unsure of what to do. Torin had been asking questions. She wasn't sure where to even begin now. Finally, she asked, "What's your name?"

"Balladyn," he said after a brief pause.

"Thanks. I didn't want to keep calling you Reaper." Breda pivoted to walk farther down the riverbank. All the while, she felt Balladyn's eyes on her.

It was an odd feeling for the Reapers to be considerate and courteous. Then again, those recruiting for the Others had been, as well. It wasn't until she was entrenched that she discovered how cruel and fanatical everyone was.

She couldn't claim to know all there was about the Reapers, and there was a good chance that what she had learned from the Others was wrong. Still, she couldn't ignore the fact that they put off an entirely different feeling.

Her thoughts moved to Torin, explaining how each of them had become Reapers. She paused and looked over her shoulder at Balladyn. The sadness she'd felt…was it because he'd been betrayed or murdered? She supposed it could be both. If it were her, she'd be bordering on homicidal instead of melancholic. It could all depend on how Balladyn had been betrayed and by who.

Breda was glad her shields hadn't slipped around Aisling or Torin. She didn't need to feel Aisling's emotions to know that the Reaper was walking a fine line unraveling at her feet. And that was just from observing her and what little conversation they'd had. One thing Breda liked about Aisling was that the female Reaper was direct. Aisling didn't beat around the bush about anything. She stated the facts—even if they were hard to hear.

Breda crossed her arms and watched the last rays of light before the sun dipped below the horizon, blanketing the realm in darkness. It had been a long while since she hadn't had something to do. She kept busy for a reason. Being still allowed her mind to drift, which tended to bring up memories she'd rather not recall.

The sound of voices got her attention. She spun around to see Torin with Balladyn. The way Torin sliced his hand through the air showed he was agitated. Breda hoped it wasn't about her. Just in case it was, she started toward them.

"...can't find her," Torin stated.

Balladyn glanced at her over Torin's shoulder. "She has to do this."

"I can't believe you just let her go."

"Would you have stopped her?" Balladyn demanded, his tone deepening.

Torin blew out a breath and sighed. "Yes. No. Fek! I don't know. I wish you would've gotten my attention so we could've both spoken to her."

"That would've only stopped her for now. She would've left later."

"You're right," Torin said with another deep sigh.

"She'll be fine. And if she isn't, she knows to call for one of us."

Torin nodded and slapped Balladyn on the shoulder. "I hope you're right." Then he turned and looked at Breda.

She winced because it looked as if she were eavesdropping. "I wasn't trying to pry. I wanted you to know I was here."

"You should've told me you needed rest," he chastised.

Balladyn walked away, saying, "Ignore him, Breda. He isn't angry at you."

Torin glanced at his friend before his gaze slid to her. "He's right. I'm angry at Aisling."

"Is she all right? Did something happen?" Breda asked.

Torin ran a hand over his jaw. "She left to take care of something."

"Are you angry because she left without telling you? Or because she didn't ask for your help?"

Torin's silver eyes met hers. He released a half-laugh, half-snort. "I think it's a bit of both."

"She seems able to take care of herself."

"She can. That doesn't mean she should be out there alone."

"If she wanted help, she would've asked," Breda pointed out.

From a distance, Balladyn let out a laugh. "I like her!"

"You're right," Torin said, ignoring Balladyn.

Breda frowned. Torin might have said he agreed with her, but his face said the opposite. "You think she's in danger?"

"The Others are hunting us. She shouldn't be out there alone."

"Maybe she'll do better because she's alone."

Torin's shoulders lifted as he drew in a deep breath and released it. "I hope you're right."

With that solved, Breda wasn't sure what to say. An uncomfortable silence ensued, and she wished Balladyn was still there since he might have filled in the quiet.

"I suppose you have more questions," she said.

He blinked at her. "Right. Questions."

"I thought you were in a hurry."

"We are," he agreed with a nod.

She swallowed nervously. "I'm ready whenever you are."

"Have you eaten?"

"I did after I woke."

"You should've told me you were tired."

She shifted uneasily. There he was, being nice again. Past experience proved that anyone who was nice wanted something from her. The fact was, she was giving him what he—and the Reapers—wanted. It shouldn't upset her that he was being pleasant.

But it did.

Maybe it had something to do with the way he had stared at her the first time they met. It was like he stripped away all the walls and blocks she had erected throughout the years. The thought that he

might have seen the scared child huddled in the corner terrified her.
She had come a long way.

And she would never go back to that place again.

She inwardly winced because she'd been that same little girl
when she hid out in the pub. What did that say about her? She
wasn't certain she wanted to find out. Then again, there was no way
to hide from who she really was.

No matter how hard she wished she could.

CHAPTER TEN

His path should be clear. Yet it wasn't. Torin knew he should focus on Breda and what she could tell him, but he couldn't stop worrying about Aisling. They all knew she had been suffering, but none of them had spoken to her about it. Mostly because they were also fiercely private.

Torin didn't want anyone in his business. Consequently, he stayed out of everyone else's. That may have been the wrong thing to do in this instance. He understood why Aisling had left to look for Xaneth. He just wished she hadn't gone alone. But she was gone, and apparently Death knew about it. That meant he should concentrate on his mission.

When he looked at Breda, she was frowning as she looked at the ground. He wanted to ask what she was thinking about, but he knew she wouldn't answer him. Instead, he asked, "What did you think of Balladyn?"

Her head jerked to him. "What? Oh. He seems nice. Didn't say too much, really."

"Is he what you expected?"

She gave him an odd look. "Why would I expect anything?"

Torin hadn't expected that answer. "Because of who he is."

"Is he different than you or Aisling or the other Reapers?"

That's when Torin knew—she had no idea who Balladyn was. And there wasn't a Dark Fae who didn't know who had once been the King of the Dark. Torin didn't call her on it right then, but he wanted to.

"I did find it curious that there is a mix of Light and Dark in the Reapers," Breda continued. "All of you get along?"

"When we become Reapers, we keep the coloring of who we were, but we're no longer Light or Dark."

Her eyes widened. "Interesting."

"What city were you recruited from?"

"Dublin."

The same place he'd found her. "And where did you do your recruiting?"

"Dublin," she said with a shrug.

"Did you ever visit the Dark Palace?"

She shook her head, her face creased in lines of denial. "Why would I go there?"

"All Light Fae see the Light Castle at least once, even if they don't go in. I know the same is true for the Dark and the Dark Palace."

"I had other things to do."

"And your family?"

In an instant, a wall came down. "I told you I didn't want to talk about my family."

"Are they involved with the Others?"

She shook her head once.

"Do they know you're involved?"

"No."

"Will the soldiers go after your family?"

Breda held his gaze. "No."

"Did the Others say anything about the previous rulers of the Dark or the Light?"

"Only in that they're happy no one has stepped into those roles. The Six plan to reign over all Fae. They want to ensure the Council that's still in its infancy fails. That way, they can step in as one cohesive unit."

He knew this already, but it was good to have confirmation from someone on the inside. "Then what?"

"You know what. They'll take out the Dragon Kings so the Fae can feast upon the mortals at will."

"That should be interesting. What of the Halflings?"

She hesitated for the barest of seconds. "The Six want them eradicated. They don't want Fae blood tainted by the mortals. They think it's repulsive."

"There are Druids."

"The Six don't recognize them as a threat."

Torin snorted. "That's unwise. The Druids shouldn't be underestimated. Neither should the Halflings."

"You asked what the plans were, and I told you."

"Walk with me," he bade her.

She fell into step with him as they strolled through the meadow with the stars twinkling overhead. The tension he had created with his query about her family slowly eased. That was a sore subject that he suspected would get him the same results no matter how many ways he asked it.

"How long did you know about the Others before you sought them out?" he asked.

She kept her gaze ahead as she said, "A few months. I kept hearing the Fae talking about them."

"Did you hear those same Fae discussing the Dark King or the Light Queen?"

Again, there was hesitation. "Of course. Why are you concerned with the King and Queen?"

"Then you know what happened to both of the rulers."

"I do."

He briefly closed his eyes at her lie. But he couldn't stop now. He had to get to the bottom of things. Otherwise, how would he know when she spoke the truth and when she didn't? "You know about the battle and how the Dark King defeated the Light Queen."

"Sure."

Torin halted and waited for her to do the same. Only when she faced him did he say, "I think it's time you came clean with the truth."

"What?" she asked, apprehension filling her gaze.

He sighed. "You've given facts about the Others we already knew. It's obvious you were in the organization."

"Then what's the problem?"

"The fact that you didn't realize Balladyn was once King of the Dark."

Her face went slack with shock. "*What?*"

"Even as a Light, I knew who ruled the Dark and my people. The Dark are the same. Why didn't you know who Balladyn was?"

Breda looked away. "Does it matter? I can give you what you want on the Others."

"I need to know if your secrets pertain to the Others—"

"They don't," she said over him. "They're private."

Torin wanted to believe her.

She shook her head and backed up a step. "Don't. Don't you dare ask."

"I have a duty to my family. You'd do the same if you were in my position."

"Everyone has secrets."

He nodded slowly. "That's true."

"I'm not asking for yours."

"If I had information you needed, I would expect you to."

She snorted as she rolled her eyes. "You're only saying that because you don't have to reveal anything."

"I told you I was betrayed and murdered. Many would consider that a significant secret. Yet I shared it without you asking."

Her lips flattened. "You didn't tell me how you were betrayed."

Torin had stepped right in front of that one. He sighed. The last thing he wanted to do was talk about the past, but he didn't have much choice if he expected Breda to do the same. He motioned for her to follow him as they retraced their steps and stopped at the grove. With a wave of his hand, he erected an elaborate tent.

He walked upon the thick carpets covering the ground and made his way to the center of the tent where a low-profile sofa in a U-shape waited. He brushed his hands over the velvet fabric in peacock blue before sitting.

Breda sat opposite him and propped her feet up on the square table that sat between them. "Do you not like nature?"

"I did this for your comfort." He pointed behind her. "There are three rooms with beds. Take your pick."

"Oh. Thank you," she said in a small voice.

Torin used his magic to call forth a twenty-five-year-old bottle of Dreagan scotch and two glasses. He poured one for himself and another for Breda and pushed it toward her. Then he sat back and took a drink. "I was a dutiful son. My family was well-off. My father owned two hotels. My mother was an accomplished singer who was paid handsomely for her performances. I was their only child. They gave me a lot of freedom and allowed me different interests. I joined the Fae Army and discovered that I was good at battle. Very good, actually. However, my parents had grand plans for me. One of which was for me to marry my father's best friend's daughter, Heda. I wasn't exactly pleased, but Heda and I got along. My parents' marriage had been arranged, and I thought if they could not only become friends but also fall in love, then I could do the same."

Breda leaned forward and grabbed the glass of whisky before sitting back.

"Heda went along with everything. At least, I thought she had. My agreeing to the arrangement backed her against a wall. While we knew each other, we weren't friends. She told me she thought I would fight the marriage because I had my duties in the army. I told her we could hold off the marriage. I wasn't in a rush. But I wasn't fighting it, either. No one knew that she had fallen in love with someone else. Or became pregnant with his child. There was no waiting for her. She wanted her life, and I was standing in her way."

Breda shrugged. "Why didn't she just tell her parents the truth?"

"They weren't like mine. They had twelve children in all, and they were controlling. Apparently, Heda refused to marry me. Her father locked her in a room. When my parents and I found out, we decided that I should talk to her. I was granted access. That's when she told me the truth. I told her that I would refuse the marriage, but she made me promise not to tell anyone about her pregnancy. We both thought me refusing would be enough. We were wrong."

Torin looked down at the glass in his hand and tossed back the whisky. "I told my parents there were circumstances that prevented the marriage. Neither pushed for answers, and my father said he'd take care of everything. He never came home. When I went looking for him, I found Heda on the street. She was crying, asking me for help. As I approached, I saw movement in the shadows. It was her father and five brothers. I fought, but I was outnumbered. I looked over to her to see her smile and walk away. With my life draining from me, her father told me how he had killed my father and mother."

"Fek," Breda said into the silence that followed. She drank the whisky, then coughed, her face wrinkled. "Why did they kill you and your parents?"

"Turns out Heda told her family I raped her. They wanted revenge. She wanted a way out, and I gave it to her."

Breda tucked her legs against her as she turned to the side. "What happened to her?"

"She ran away with her lover. They had four kids before he left her for someone else."

"Ouch. Did you ever seek revenge?"

He lifted one shoulder in a shrug. "All Reapers think about it, but we don't do it. We're given a second chance. Granted, we never forget what happened to us, but we don't wallow in the past."

"That's shite."

"Oh?"

"You have a tremendous amount of pain and anger within you."

He jerked at her words. "How would you know that?"

Breda lowered her gaze to the glass in her hands. "Just a guess."

"You were pretty specific. How do you know?"

"I can feel it," she finally admitted.

Torin scooted to the edge of the cushion and caught her gaze. "Are you telling me you're an empath?"

"I have blocks up, but sometimes, things get through. Your voice was even and calm through the story, but your feelings were…overwhelming."

"Bloody hell."

CHAPTER ELEVEN

The need to bolt, to hide, was strong. Somehow, Breda remained on the sofa. She couldn't hold Torin's gaze, however. She hadn't meant to tell him that his emotions had flooded her shields. The words had tumbled from her lips before she could stop them.

It had been a very long time since someone had gotten through her defenses without even trying. Torin's voice had belied his true opinions. But his feelings had made them crystal-clear. She wouldn't have guessed to look at him that he was holding in so much pain and anger.

"An empath," Torin mumbled.

She turned the glass around in her hands. Breda wished he didn't know. She wished she didn't have the power. It had been nothing but a hindrance.

Torin slowly sat back. "You don't like your ability?"

"My curse, you mean?"

"Some would disagree."

"Those would be the people who don't know what it's like to be born with such an affliction. They don't know how horrible life can be, especially when they don't know how to stop being overwhelmed by the feelings of others around them."

There was sadness in Torin's silver eyes. "Is that what happened to you?"

It was worse. So much worse. Breda didn't want to talk about it. Her past was better left unspoken, but she didn't have that option. He had shared his with her. Now, it was her turn.

"I'm not here to judge," he told her.

She moved her head from side to side, popping her neck. Then she set the glass on the table and cracked each finger before getting to her feet and shaking out her hands. Every nerve was wired, buzzing with anxiety and distress. She had to move, so she began pacing behind the sofa she had been sitting on. "I don't talk about my past."

"Neither do I."

Shite. She really wasn't going to get out of this. Breda glanced at Torin to find him watching her. "What happens if you hear something you don't like?"

His expression remained neutral. "As I said, I'm not here to judge."

"You might feel differently once you know everything."

"If you knew the things I had witnessed, you wouldn't say that."

"But I don't know the things you've seen."

Torin caught her gaze and held it. "Breda. Just tell your story."

"Fek." She covered her face with he hands as she continued pacing. When she let her arms fall to her sides, she fisted her hands, hoping it would help with the rising storm. "I had eleven siblings. I was number nine. My mother was…strict. Cruel beyond imagining. She was mentally, emotionally, and physically abusive. But not to all of us. Just the one she hated. Me."

Breda paused and put her hand on the back of the sofa to steady herself. She had never said the words aloud. Giving them a voice brought it all back as if it were still happening. She had left that life years ago, but the memories could yank her back in an instant.

"My siblings learned quickly that if they spoke to me or offered me any type of kindness, she retaliated. I was in a house full of people, and yet I was utterly and completely alone. It was a horrible feeling. Nothing I said, nothing I did was ever right. If I spoke, she hit me. If I was quiet, she hit me. The mere sight of me sent her into a rage. She kept me locked in a tiny closet so she didn't have to see me. She would forget to bring me food or water—sometimes for days. My two younger sisters snuck me food when they could, but more often than not, I went hungry."

"Fek me."

She startled at the sound of Torin's voice laced with fury. Her head swung to him to find him sitting forward once more, concern lining his face. She squeezed her eyes shut and turned her back to him.

She took a deep breath and continued. "The only relief I had was when my grandmother visited. She would take me out of the closet and give me all kinds of food. She would often offer me some kind of doll or other present. I was so starved for attention that even though I knew what was coming, I still climbed onto her lap and let her hug me and comb my hair."

There was a beat of silence. "What did you know was coming?"

Breda opened her eyes to look at the deep blue fabric of the tent. But she was back in her mother's home, sitting on her grandmother's lap. "She used me. Took me out and put me near someone who was experiencing heavy emotions—all kinds of emotions. Rage, hate, sorrow, loneliness, jealousy, disgust, shame, guilt. Never happiness. Never anything…*good*. As a child, you don't have concepts of such emotions. Not the way adults feel them. My grandmother got great pleasure seeing me overwhelmed by others' feelings. It felt like I was drowning. I would reach for her, begging for help, but she would only back away while wearing a smile.

"When she finished playing with me, she would return me to my closet, and I would be left alone to deal with whatever emotions assaulted me. I would cry and curl into a ball as I promised myself that I would never accept her gifts again. But after weeks of being locked in the closet, the door would finally open, and she would smile down at me and hold out her hand. I took it."

"You were a child," Torin said in a soft voice. "You can't be angry at yourself for needing attention. I don't know many adults who would have withstood what you did."

Breda shook her head as she leaned her hips back to rest against the sofa, her hands braced on either side of her. She took a deep breath, feeling it wobble within her. "During the day, I could hear my siblings and my mother. I couldn't see them, but at least I could hear what was going on. The nights were the hardest because there was only silence. I tried to pick the lock and leave once. I had my arm broken in two places when Mum found me. She didn't want me there, but she wouldn't let me leave. While my siblings went to school and learned, I remained behind. I heard them practicing spells and magic. One time, I tried one of the spells and it worked. Unfortunately, Mum was nearby and realized what I had done. After that, none of my siblings did magic anywhere I could hear."

"Take this."

She looked down to find a glass filled with whisky in Torin's hand. Her gaze traveled up his arm to his face. She hadn't heard him get up. "What?"

"Drink," he urged.

It would dull the memories, and that could only be a good thing. Breda accepted the drink and took a sip, then another. And another. When her body was flush with the alcohol, she gradually released a breath.

"How long did you endure such abuse?"

She glanced at Torin and shrugged. "I knew that if I didn't get out, I would be there until she killed me. That was her plan, I believe. I don't know how old I was when I finally told myself that I would get free or die trying. Most of my siblings were already out of the house. There were only a few of us left. I continued trying to do magic during the night when everyone slept. I still remember how easy it was to unlock the door. It swung open quietly, and I crawled out. My clothes were dirty and too small, but I wasn't concerned about my appearance. I saw freedom, and I was going to take it. I walked softly to the back door and turned the knob. I didn't know that she had set a spell on it to warn her if anyone opened it. I heard her moving upstairs, and I ran. I ran as fast as my legs could carry me. I had nowhere to go, no money, and no idea of the world, but it was better than where I had been."

"Then what happened?" Torin asked as he leaned on the back of the sofa beside her.

"I lived on the streets of Dublin, scrounging for food. I thought I was safe. My grandmother found me, however. She threatened to call for Mum unless I did something for her. I thought she wanted me to experience emotions again. She did, sort of. Hers. I didn't know what she planned. I was wholly unprepared for the visceral hate that assaulted me. I didn't know how to take it and channel it. Instead, it consumed me so that her emotions became mine. Next thing I knew, I had killed my grandmother's rival. She laughed and hugged me, told me how good I had done. I knew it was wrong that I had taken a life, but no one had ever praised me before. She kept saying that she always knew I had it in me to be a strong Dark. I was numb, but she took me home with her. She clothed me, fed me, and began teaching me more magic. It felt so good to have someone looking after me. She encouraged me, praised me. Then, every few weeks, she would drown me in more of her emotions, and I would take another life."

Torin swallowed loudly. "How long did this last?"

"A few years. Until I tried to run. She called for my mum. I reacted without thinking and—and…"

"You killed her."

Breda nodded slowly as she looked at him. "I didn't mean to. I didn't want to."

"You were fighting for your life. No one would hold that against you. You certainly shouldn't."

"How can I not?"

His shoulders lifted as he inhaled. "Forgive yourself. That's the only way you can move on."

"You make it sound easy."

"It isn't. What happened after you got away from your grandmother?"

Breda pulled the hair tie that held her hair atop her head. Her locks fell around her shoulders. "I'd learned enough to make my way. And I listened. I'd sit in places like the Sly Stag and move from table to table, eavesdropping on the Fae around me. Sometimes, I spoke to a few. That's how I learned about putting up shields to keep others' emotions out. That made a huge difference. I could walk down the street without being brought to my knees by someone's emotions. And that pretty much brings us to now."

He grunted. "I'm sorry you suffered so, but your strength shows in what you've endured and how you've come out ahead."

"I suppose."

"But you still haven't told me your secret," he said as he turned his head to her.

Breda looked into his eyes. She had come this far. She might as well tell the rest. "My mum had an affair with a human and got pregnant with me. She wanted to kill me at birth, but my grandmother somehow knew that I was an empath and told my mum to keep me alive so they could use me later."

"You're a Halfling?" Torin asked in shock.

She nodded.

Torin pushed away from the sofa and walked a few steps forward before spinning to face her. "But you look like a Dark. Your hair and eyes changed. What were your hair and eye color before?"

"Like yours," she told him.

"Some Halflings do have the coloring of a Light, but I've never known one to change."

She shrugged, not at all as intrigued by the situation as he was. "How many of them have committed murder?"

He strode to her, his eyes once more intense as he locked on hers. "They manipulated you into that. Had you known how to put up shields, your grandmother never would've been able to put you in that position. None of this is your fault, Breda. None of it."

The last thing she should've done was look too deeply into his silver depths. She saw things she wanted to see, not what was actually there. And that could be detrimental for her.

CHAPTER TWELVE

Torin took an immediate step back from Breda the instant he found himself wanting to lower his head and press his lips to hers. Too many people had used her, and he didn't want her to think that's what he was doing.

Although, that's precisely what he and the other Reapers *were* doing.

Her story had moved him, but something in her voice and the way she held her body had struck a chord deep within him. Breda had been well acquainted with betrayal on a level that most couldn't comprehend. Yet, she hadn't let the darkness she had lived hand in hand with for so long consume her. She had found a different path, one that suited her.

It might not have been the best journey, but it was a different one. There were so many other roads she could've taken. He couldn't say for certain if he would've had her strength. It would've been a lot easier for her to let the darkness in. Breda had stood against it, daring it to intrude again.

And it had—with the Others.

He took in her face, the innocence somehow still there despite the horrors she had endured. The light within her was strong and steady, overtaking the darkness. Despite the times people had betrayed her, she had opened herself and put her trust in him. Now that he knew her story, he was shocked. And astonished.

Torin cleared his throat. He had to take his mind off her mouth and his desire to kiss her. "How have you passed in the Fae world as a Halfling? A Fae knows other Fae."

"How do you pick out Halflings?" she asked with a tilt of her head.

He shrugged. "We sense it."

"But you realize they don't have all the magic of the Fae. Hence, a Halfling."

"Aye. So, why didn't I sense you were one?"

"Because I'm not. Not really." She wrinkled her nose. "My father wasn't only human. He was a Halfling. I have a quarter human blood. The rest is Fae."

The way her eyes searched his only caused him to be more aware of her allure. She was an enticement he didn't want or need. She looked to him for protection against the Others. That's what he would give her. He wanted her to know that she could trust someone, that he could be nice, and not expect her to do something in return.

"Your silence is freaking me out."

He inwardly shook himself. "I was thinking. No wonder you passed with three-quarters Fae blood. Would that have held up under scrutiny?"

"You mean if the Six had questioned me?" She shrugged. "I don't know. And, frankly, I don't want to ever find out."

Torin nodded in agreement. "It's not the fact that you aren't full-blooded Fae that makes me want to keep you out of the Others' hands."

"It's because I'm an empath."

"You know how it feels to be manipulated by emotions as a child. I don't think you want to find out how it feels as an adult."

She bit her lip. "I've got shields in place. Not to mention, I'm stronger with my magic now than before."

"Your defenses slipped."

"It won't happen again," she stated.

"You know better than any of us what the Six are like. Do you think they would learn of your power and not use it?"

Breda straightened and looked around helplessly. "I didn't ask to be an empath. I didn't want it."

"But you have the power. We might be overthinking. If the soldiers don't find you—which they won't here—then they'll never learn what power you hold. Unless…"

Her brows snapped together. "Unless what?"

He didn't want to say it. Didn't want to bring it up. But he had no choice. They had to think of everything. "What if your family tells them?"

"They won't," she said dismissively.

"Are they dead?"

"No."

"Then there's always a chance."

"They've forgotten about me by now."

They both knew that was a lie, but Torin didn't press her on it—not now, at least.

She absently ran her fingers along the shaved side of her head. "You and Aisling vowed to do whatever was necessary to keep me out of the Others' hands. I'm going to hold you to it."

Torin bowed his head to her. "There's nothing that could stop me from keeping that vow."

"Good. I think I'm going to go rest. The enticement to sleep an entire night is too much to resist."

He stepped aside and motioned to the three curtains that were pulled back. "Choose whichever room you want."

She stopped at the first one and peeked inside before continuing to the second and doing the same. After a look in the third, she ducked behind the curtain. A second later, there was a whoosh as they closed.

Torin waited for another moment before he turned on his heel and walked outside. He was still shaken by her story. A part of him wasn't surprised when Balladyn came around from the rear of the tent. The two met and silently made their way to the river.

"You heard?" Torin asked.

Balladyn nodded.

Torin wondered why the former King wouldn't look him in the eye, then he realized that Balladyn must have heard his story, as well.

"I'm sorry," Balladyn replied. "I should've walked away when you spoke of your past."

"Why? I know yours. Isn't it only fair you know mine?"

Balladyn shrugged. "Fair isn't a word I speak of often. I no longer think it applies anymore."

"We don't talk about what made us Reapers because we want to forget. Maybe that's the problem. We shouldn't forget. We should embrace it."

Balladyn's eyebrows shot up on his forehead. "I wonder if you would've thought that before speaking with Breda."

"I don't know," Torin admitted. "Probably not."

"She has a way about her. I wouldn't call her calming because she's a bundle of raw nerves, but then she'll look at you as if she sees you clearly."

"Because she feels the emotions we hide. Even from ourselves."

Balladyn looked into the distance. "I think she felt mine earlier. She didn't admit it, but she acted differently."

"What did she sense?"

Instead of answering, Balladyn turned his head to him. "She's powerful. I don't think she realizes the full extent of her ability. She has kept below anyone's attention, which is a miracle in itself. But she isn't strong enough to stand against more commanding Fae like us."

"Or the Others," Torin added.

"She can be taught ways, but even then, I'm not sure it'll be enough. Breda has made her way, but many aspects of her are naïve."

Torin glanced at the tent. "She's made it this far."

"What about her family?"

"You heard what she said."

"And you know it's shite. Are they part of the Others? Have they been recruited? Will they go to the soldiers and alert them that they know Breda and what she is?"

Torin shrugged. "I don't know."

"We should be proactive in that regard."

Torin rubbed a hand over the back of his neck. "Shite. She won't tell me anything about her family."

"We don't need her," Balladyn said with a grin.

Torin nodded in agreement.

"I'm going to put up some protection around the doorway from Earth so we'll be alerted if anyone comes through," Balladyn said before he teleported.

Torin pivoted to stare at the tent, his mind going over Breda's story again. He thought about the first time he had seen her and how he couldn't put his finger on what was different about her. Even now, he wasn't sure if it was because she was only three-quarters Fae or if it was because she was an empath.

It was rare for a Fae to have such power. Many humans had the ability, although few understood it or knew what to do with it. He found it odd that mortals were afraid of things they didn't understand. Instead of searching for what caused someone to suffer like an empath who had no idea they were one, they let their symptoms manifest into other things or took pills hoping they would make them *normal*. And when it didn't work, they took more and more drugs. All the humans needed was for someone to tell them that they were empaths and teach them what that meant.

Torin rubbed his chest. There had been a knot of emotion there since he had been betrayed and murdered. The burden of his parents' deaths had weighed heavily upon him for centuries. Oddly, though, he felt a little lighter.

Could it be because he'd shared his story? He had never spoken about it with anyone. He didn't even like to think of it because it made him realize how trusting he had been. He mourned his parents' needless murder. They had all been caught up in Heda's lies and deceptions. For a long time, Torin had wanted revenge. He was glad he'd never taken it.

Balladyn reappeared. "The protection veil is up."

"I'd like to think we have all the time in the world to get information from Breda, but we don't. With Aisling out there alone, we need to make sure the Others can't find her or any Reaper."

Balladyn crossed his arms over his chest. "This is when I wonder why Death doesn't reap the souls of the Six. I know more would step in, but after a while, the Fae would get the hint, and no one would take the positions."

"Hmm. It's a nice thought. Then it would make us into the monsters the Six claim we are."

"Erith keeps the balance between good and evil. Unfortunately, nothing is more balanced than the Others. Three Light, three Dark."

Torin released a long breath. "I wouldn't want the power Erith has. Cael tried to describe how different things were for him after taking some of her power and becoming a god. Erith has much to consider. It's why she tries to stay neutral."

"She's going to want to talk to Breda."

"I know. I wanted to let Breda rest for the night. Morning is soon enough for us to introduce her to Erith."

Balladyn's head turned to him. "What about you?"

"What about me?"

"You have a connection with Breda."

Torin shrugged one shoulder. "Aisling and I found her, we took her from the soldiers, and we vowed we would keep her from the Others—even taking her life as a last resort. With Aisling's attention on other things, I had to step in since it was our mission."

"I wasn't judging."

"Then what was your comment?"

Balladyn dropped his arms to his sides. "Tell me why you keep looking at the tent."

"We're protecting her."

"There isn't anything here."

Torin quirked a brow. "Not now, there isn't."

"She's pretty. There's no harm in noticing that."

"All Fae are attractive."

Balladyn's lips curved in a smile. "When was the last time you had fun? What about Breda? When did she have fun just to have it?"

"How am I to know that?" he snapped.

"We need more information about the Others. Instead of drilling her on the sofa in the tent, take her out to see more of the realm. Let her enjoy the beauty and safety while she can. Hell, we all should. It could all come crashing down tomorrow."

Torin stared after Balladyn long after the former King of the Dark walked away. Then Torin's gaze moved to the tent. Balladyn was right. Breda did need to have fun.

CHAPTER THIRTEEN

Dublin

Aisling walked the streets of the city, searching each face for Xaneth. It was a longshot that he was here, but she hadn't known where else to begin. The Reapers as a group couldn't track him. Neither could Cael, nor Erith. Aisling wasn't sure why she thought she would be able to find him when the others couldn't.

It wasn't just the repercussions from Death Aisling would have to deal with when this was over. There was also the Six and their soldiers. The Others were getting close to being able to track the Reapers, and the last thing Aisling wanted was to be caught alone. Sooner or later, she would have to battle the soldiers, but she would rather do it with her fellow Reapers.

That was if Death didn't expel her for disobeying an order.

The feeling inside Aisling wasn't one she could ignore any longer. She barely understood it, which made trying to describe it to anyone else nearly impossible. Yet, she would have to find the words eventually because once she had to face Erith, she would only have one chance to explain herself.

At least, she hoped she got the chance.

Aisling didn't want to think about that yet. There would be plenty of time for those thoughts later. For now, she needed to concentrate on Xaneth. It wasn't a coincidence that he had found the soldiers both at the field and on Achill Island where Rordan had been.

She had seen the Fae accomplish some amazing feats—both Dark and Light—before she became a Reaper. But what Xaneth did exceeded all of that. If she didn't know better, she would think he was a Reaper. But Death would've told them if that were the case. Yet, the force of his magic, his lethal battle skills, and the way he attacked as if he didn't care if he lived or died told her that something drove him.

He was on a mission. And it was one she knew in her gut he couldn't continue alone. Only someone with a death wish acted like Xaneth.

The thought drew her up short. She ducked into an alley and pressed her back against the brick. Thunder cracked before the skies opened with the storm. She didn't bother to run inside or shield herself from the rain. Her mind was too preoccupied. No one knew what kind of torture Usaeil had inflicted upon Xaneth, but everyone understood that it had been horrendous. The fact that Xaneth lived was a miracle in itself.

Aisling had seen true evil, had felt it. And Usaeil had embodied the same malevolence, the same malice.

The same need to hurt. Destroy.

And to kill.

Usaeil's moral compass—if she'd ever had one—had been ruined. Nothing would have prevented her from unleashing the cruelest, nastiest suffering she could imagine. The fact that Xaneth was still alive spoke to his strength. But even someone as mentally and physically strong as Xaneth had a breaking point.

For all Aisling knew, his mind was broken.

Raindrops dripped from her lashes onto her cheeks. She blinked them away as she tried to imagine where she would go if she were him. He appeared to be after the soldiers. Since she and Torin had found Breda in Dublin, and the soldiers had come after Breda at the

Sly Stag, Xaneth could be there searching for clues as to where the soldiers would go next.

"Or I could be wasting my time," she mumbled to herself.

Dublin was a big city. She could search for weeks and never find Xaneth. She didn't have that kind of time. Balladyn had said that he would keep silent about her leaving, but for how long? She didn't want anyone taking heat for her decision. Which meant she had to believe that she only had a few hours before Death, Cael, or Eoghan came for her.

She pushed away from the wall and veiled herself before teleporting outside the Sly Stag. Aisling watched the door for several minutes, noting the many Fae who came and went. The few glimpses she got inside when the door opened made it appear as if everything were back to normal. She could drop her veil and go inside, but there were benefits to being a Reaper—advantages she might not have for much longer. It was better if she used them now rather than waiting.

After twenty minutes, she followed a group inside the pub. One Fae bumped into her, but she quickly moved away. The male looked around to see who he'd hit, then shrugged when he couldn't see anyone. As a Reaper, being able to stay veiled as long as she wanted was a boon—especially since no other Fae could.

Aisling moved around the pub with relative ease. She looked at each face but couldn't find Xaneth. Then she turned to the back rooms. She knew there was a slim chance he would be there, but she had to try because she didn't know where to go from here.

She teleported from room to room, wincing at some of the sights she saw. When she reached the room that Breda had been in, she jumped inside, not thinking to find anything. The shock that went through her at finding Xaneth made her knees go weak.

He sat on the end of the bed, bent over with his forearms resting on his knees. His head snapped up, and he looked directly at her. Aisling knew that he couldn't see her. Only another Reaper could discern her. Yet there was no question that Xaneth looked at *her*.

≈

The Dungeon

Water dripped incessantly behind the wall that Ruarc leaned against. He had paced the tiny cell for days, not that he moved much. He couldn't take three full steps in any direction. He had just enough room to lay down, but he preferred not to recline upon the dirty, wet stones.

He had no idea where he was, other than some ancient dungeon that hadn't seen daylight in thousands of years.

He had no idea who had taken him, though he had an inkling it had something to do with the meetings he'd been forced to attend on Achill Island.

He had no idea why he had been taken because no one would tell him.

Then again, he hadn't seen anyone to ask since he had been hit from behind with magic and woke up in the dungeon. Surely, someone would eventually come for him, if for no other reason than to flaunt all the reasons above.

Ruarc wondered how Rordan had done with Fianna and her family. What little time Ruarc had spent with Rordan showed that once the Fae had a plan, he didn't deviate. Ruarc wished he had been there to see it because he had a feeling that Rordan triumphed.

He crouched down on his haunches and rubbed the back of his neck. He had tried magic dozens of times, but nothing budged the lock or the iron door. He had called out to Rordan, but the Fae had never appeared. Doubt crept in that Rordan hadn't come because he didn't want to, not because he couldn't hear Ruarc.

Ruarc had no idea how long he had been in the dungeon. He might not have been a saint, but he didn't deserve this. What worried him was that he couldn't use his magic. No Fae should have been able to hold him this long. Something in his magic should've showed a chink in the warding being used, but it hadn't. He wasn't the strongest Fae, but he wasn't the weakest, either. He should've been able to get out.

That led his thoughts to Fianna's brother, Dorcha, and the meetings he had run to recruit Fae. Something about the entire event had been off. Rordan had expressed doubt about them. As much as Dorcha wanted everyone to think that he ran the show, Ruarc knew that wasn't the truth. Dorcha was merely a pawn.

Then who was in charge?

Ruarc's head jerked to the door when it suddenly swung open with a loud squeal. Two male Fae dressed in black stood before him —one Light, one Dark. Just like the Fae at Dorcha's house that had seemed entirely out of place. These two were the same. They may look like Fae, but there was something different about them. Something Ruarc instinctively wanted to avoid.

"Come," the Dark ordered.

Ruarc slowly straightened. "Why?"

"You've been summoned," the Light answered.

"By whom?" Ruarc asked.

Neither answered as they reached for him simultaneously. Ruarc stepped back, ready to attack with his fists if he had to. But they moved so quickly that he didn't have time to do anything before they had a hold of him. He decided to play along for the moment. Maybe he would get answers now. At the very least, he would get to see how deep he was underground and if there were other prisoners.

The narrow hallway barely left room for the three of them to walk. They passed several closed doors on each side. Ruarc counted two open doors. He wondered if those who had been within had been summoned as he had.

Or if they were dead.

He tried not to think of the latter, but it was difficult. Since he was no longer close with his family, no one would miss him. No one would even know that he was gone, much less worry about him. He got a good look at his life, and he didn't like it. He might tell himself that it wasn't his fault, but he'd had a hand in it.

His father might have put the family in the difficult position that had caused Ruarc to make questionable decisions, but no one had forced him. He'd made those choices all on his own. He could've walked away, could have chosen another path, but he hadn't. He had continued to walk the one that he'd known spelled destruction.

Maybe that's what he wanted subconsciously. He'd been lonely and miserable for some time. The few times he'd contemplated making a change, he had been dragged back by his family's promise to make right what they had done wrong. Yet it wasn't anyone but Ruarc making the sacrifices. He'd taken the weight of everyone on himself, believing he had to shoulder it all when he should've distributed it to others.

Actually, his sire should've done that, proving once again that his father wasn't the man he proclaimed himself to be.

Maybe that was why Ruarc liked to stay under the radar. He didn't make a spectacle of himself, and he wasn't interested in a lot of attention. If he said that he would do something, he made sure to do it.

Ruarc's thoughts halted when he and his two guards reached a narrow set of stairs. He was surprised that they didn't teleport and instead shoved him forward. The steep incline confirmed the age of the structure. When he reached the top, he tried to look around, but the guards quickly took his arms and roughly turned him to the left down an arched corridor. There were no paintings or décor upon the walls, just simple lights floating above them to illuminate the way.

The hallway went on for some time before he was taken to the right, then the left, and finally one more right before they halted before a set of modern double doors that looked out of place against the backdrop of the ancient structure he had been led through.

The guards released him and stepped back. Ruarc glanced at them, but neither looked in his direction. He drew in a deep breath and slowly released it as he moved closer to the doors. Just as he was about to touch them, they opened. He had no idea how big the room was because it was pitch black, except for a raised, round dais where six individuals stood in a circle beneath bright lights—three Dark and three Light. Five women and one male wearing blinding white robes.

Everything within Ruarc told him to run. He tried to call his magic. Hope shot through him when he felt it answer. Before he could form an orb of protection, though, he was in the middle of the circle of Fae. Icy fear ran down his spine. Without having to be told, he halted his magic. Ruarc looked at each of them as he slowly turned in a circle.

"You were going to turn your back on us."

Ruarc jerked his head to the Light female who had spoken. She stood between two other Light Fae. Something about her looked familiar. "I don't know who you are."

She smiled, though it held no mirth. "Oh, but you do."

CHAPTER FOURTEEN

"You want to do what?" Breda asked Torin the next morning.

He smiled, his gaze daring her to back down. "Are you afraid?"

"I came with you to another realm. I'm not scared," she retorted. But it was a lie. She had no idea what he had up his sleeve, and he obviously had something planned. She didn't like surprises.

"Good," he replied. "Let's go."

She glanced around. "What about Balladyn?"

"He has other things to do," Torin said as he started walking.

Breda rolled her eyes and followed him. She had risen that morning thinking she would be talking about the Others again. Before she had been able to tell him that she was ready to start, he had told her they were going for a walk. She shouldn't have been defensive, but years of being on guard had caused her to react before she thought about it.

They walked in silence for a time. It wasn't long before she stopped worrying what Torin's motives were and began enjoying the scenery. She saw flocks of bright yellow birds in the distance. She heard the calls of some big cat mixed in with various songbirds. The wind was light, the rays of the sun warm. All of it lulled her.

She realized that she was content for the first time in her life.

She wasn't afraid, wasn't on guard. Torin knew her story and her secrets. All of that, combined with the fact that the soldiers couldn't find her, allowed her to breathe easier. Her gaze briefly slid to Torin. Just like when she'd met him, his presence eased her anxiety.

Of course, it could be that she felt so good because she had slept like the dead.

Yes, it had to be the sleep. She looked at Torin again, her eyes moving over his rigid jawline and the inky strands of his hair that ruffled in the breeze. Was he handsome? Absolutely. She was glad that he was a Reaper and out of her reach because given how he made her feel, she might never want to leave him.

Her fingers brushed the tall grass, the bark of the trees, flowers, and anything else close. She was awed at the easy feeling within her. She had lived with fear and anxiety for so long that she had forgotten what it felt like not to have it. And she was going to enjoy every second of it while she could.

She followed Torin up a hill before they climbed a taller, steeper incline after that. The higher they went, the more she could see of the realm. From her vantage point, she saw over the treetops in the valley. She stopped and took in a distant rain shower, watching as the thick sheets of water fell from the clouds. She saw small, bright blue birds hopping around on outstretched limbs, and large white cranes that lazily flapped their wings as they glided from one tree to the next.

Breda didn't know how long she stood taking it all in before she remembered that Torin was there. Her head snapped to the side to find him about ten steps away, watching the birds, too.

He turned his head to her and raised a brow as his lips curved slightly. He was asking her if she was ready to continue. No one had ever given such thought to her before. A part of her wanted to push him and see if he would be willing to remain, but another part of her wanted to see what else there was.

She nodded, and they started walking again. Breda liked that he didn't talk. She was lost in her thoughts, drifting from one to another like hopping on stones across a river. She pretended that she was a different person, with a different life—safe and loved. It was a beautiful fiction. One she had created since she was a little girl locked in the closet.

Breda had believed that once she was on her own, she would have that life. That was the cruelest part of all because that fantasy had helped her hold on when there was nothing else to cling to. Yet, she learned quickly enough that life was arduous, unsympathetic, and brutal. Almost as nasty as those who inhabited the realm.

Somehow, she survived all of it, only to find herself on a beautiful realm with a gorgeous Fae, sheltered and...happy.

Torin suddenly stopped. She halted and found his eyes pointed upward. Breda followed his gaze to the mountain before them.

He looked at her. "We can jump to the top, or we could climb."

Breda slid her gaze from him to the mountain and inwardly cringed. There was one more secret she hadn't shared. It was minor, at least that's what she told herself. "Let's climb."

He shot her a bright smile that made her breath catch. Her stomach quivered. She'd never felt anything like it before. She quickly looked away. But she could still see his face in her mind's eye. The crinkling of his eyes at the corners, the way the sun reflected off his silver irises, the excitement filling his face. No one had ever reacted in such a way to anything she had done.

Torin had been nothing but honest and open from the moment they met. She wanted to put up walls and continue thinking that he was like everyone else, but she knew that wasn't true. Deep down, in some secret part of herself, she knew that he wasn't faking anything she had just seen. He was *truly* excited.

To be with her, to share the moment *with her*.

"Breda?"

Her eyes closed. Why did he have to say her name like it was a caress? A sweet seduction that promised not only pleasure but also utter fulfillment. Her blood heated, and her heart began to thump in her chest. Her lips parted as she fought to catch her breath.

She shouldn't let her mind think such thoughts. Torin was off-limits.

Wasn't he?

Her eyes opened. Who ever said she couldn't have some fun?

There was no telling how much longer she would live. The soldiers would never stop hunting her, and while she knew Torin and Aisling would uphold their vows, they were also being pursued.

Breda turned to Torin. It was on the tip of her tongue to tell him everything running through her mind, to reach for him and kiss him.

His smile was gone. Concern filled his face now. "You okay?"

She hesitated, losing her nerve. "Just thinking about the climb. Mind if I go first?"

He grinned and backed away. "Be my guest."

She smoothed her fingers through her hair and wound the strands into a bun that she secured with a hair tie as she pulled her thoughts from Torin to the climb. Then she ran her fingers along the shaved sides of her head and around to the back as she searched the mountain for just the right place to start. When she found it, she used magic to change her clothes to something better suited to climbing.

Flashing a grin at Torin, she got a good toe and handhold before launching herself up. The climb was strenuous. It challenged her body and mind—and she loved every second. Now she understood why humans dared such feats. At least if she fell, she could use magic to prevent injury and death. Mortals couldn't, and yet they continued to free-climb.

By the time she reached the top, she had never felt so exhilarated. She jumped up, spreading her arms as she released a loud yell of excitement. She spun around to find Torin pulling himself to the summit. She couldn't contain her smile.

He met her gaze as he straightened. "Climbing suits you."

"It does," she agreed with a laugh. "I never would've thought that."

"Then you'll appreciate that even more," he said as he jerked his chin to something over her shoulder.

Breda turned and saw the lake in the valley below. The water was so clear and blue that it didn't look real. Even from their height, she could see the bottom of the lakebed. Beautiful didn't begin to describe the scene before her.

"Race you," Torin said.

He rushed past her. "Hey! Wait!" she called as she started running to catch up with him.

His longer legs ate up the distance. She could've used magic to beat him, but she didn't. His laughter filled the air, and it wasn't long before hers joined in. She felt free, so completely uninhibited that she thought she could've flown.

Several times, her feet nearly tangled on the way down to the valley. She wasn't far behind Torin but enough that she knew when to jump over logs or dodge boulders. The shoreline was fast approaching, but neither of them pulled up. Breda pumped her legs faster in a last-ditch effort to catch Torin.

He glanced at her, their gazes meeting as their smiles widened. She didn't want him to pull up to let her win, and thankfully, he didn't. With the water's edge coming closer and closer, they ran faster until they reached the water and slowed.

Breda tripped and pitched forward into the lake. She broke the surface, laughing so hard her cheeks hurt. For several minutes, she and Torin sat in the shallow water, laughing until it died away when her eyes took in the way his wet shirt molded to the hard muscles of his chest. Suddenly, her stomach was full of butterflies as her nerve endings prickled.

The heat from earlier was back with a vengeance, and this time, it wasn't going away.

He blinked water from his lashes and raked his hands through his hair to get it off his face. His gaze lowered, and she realized that he was staring at her breasts through her white shirt. There were many reasons Breda should halt all the lascivious, lurid thoughts in her head.

And so many, many more why she shouldn't.

Usually, her curiosity ruled her. This time, it was her body. She crawled to him, never breaking eye contact. His hands closed around her when she reached him, pulling her against him as he lay back in the shallow water.

The feel of him pressed along her body was…everything. And more. Her heart hammered erratically. Her blood pounded in her

ears. All because she wanted nothing but to taste Torin. She splayed
her hand on his chest and felt the hard sinew through his shirt. His
arousal pressed against her stomach. She drew in a shaky breath,
praying this wasn't a dream.

Neither said a word as their heads slowly moved toward the
other. Just before their lips brushed, her eyelids closed. His mouth
was soft as he kissed her once, twice, three times before lingering
longer. The fourth time his lips parted against hers, softly seeking,
sampling, tasting. She melted against him, their tongues tangling as
he rolled her toward shore and kissed her deeply, thoroughly.

Completely.

His hand ran up her side, moving beneath her shirt to her bare
skin. As he caressed upward, their clothes vanished. The kiss
deepened as their passion intensified and consumed them. She ran
her hands over his back and shoulders, glorying in the feel of his
muscles moving beneath her palms.

There was only Torin—his hands, his body.

His mouth.

He ended the kiss as he moved between her legs as water lapped
at her calves. Her eyes opened to find him staring. He bent and
closed his mouth around her nipple, suckling as he held her gaze.
Her sex clenched, eager to feel him inside her.

She reached between them and found him. Her lips parted
when her hand moved up and down his length. The more he
suckled, the more she pumped her hand on his cock until neither of
them could stand it anymore.

Torin entered her in one thrust. She cried out, grabbing hold of
him as their bodies finally joined. Then he began moving. Water
slapped loudly against them. She pulled his head down for a kiss as
passion rose swiftly. As if he knew, he thrust deeper, harder. Faster.

The climax took her unawares. It flung her high, her body
pulsing with ecstasy. She embraced it, reached for it, and was
rewarded with waves upon waves of bliss rolling through her. Just
when she didn't think she could take any more, Torin buried himself
deep in her with a final thrust, tossing her back into the sea of
pleasure.

CHAPTER FIFTEEN

Things were so simple when there was peace. If only Torin could remain that way. But it wasn't to be.

He swam lazily in the lake as Breda sunned on the shore. It was only when she had drifted off to sleep that he untangled himself from her limbs and slipped beneath the water. He paused and looked back at the beach, a smile on his face to see her beautiful body.

Her chest rose as she took a deep breath and lifted her arms above her head in a stretch. He treaded water, waiting for her to sit. After a moment, she bent one leg to tuck it beneath her as she sat and placed her other foot on the ground with her knee bent. She scanned the area, only stopping when she found him.

She smiled and waved before rising to her feet. He gazed upon her hourglass figure, lingering on her breasts. Torin quickly swam back to her. He took her hand and tried to pull her into the lake, but she resisted.

"I won't let anything happen to you."

Her gaze dropped to the water. "I'm fine here."

"You'll climb a mountain, but you won't swim?"

She shrugged. "Something like that."

"Use your magic. You won't drown." He saw her vacillating as she contemplated his words.

Her lips pressed together as she frowned.

"You can hold onto me. And if you get scared, you can teleport to shore."

She wrinkled her nose and then sighed loudly. "I might pass as a Fae, but I can't teleport."

He blinked, shocked—and slightly angered. "Why in the world did you climb the mountain then? You could've fallen."

"I would've used other magic."

He motioned his fingers in a come-hither gesture with his outstretched hand. "If you can climb that mountain, you can swim."

"When you put it that way, I can't exactly refuse."

"Precisely," he replied with a grin.

Her hand slipped into his. The farther she walked into the water, the tighter she held onto him. He moved her hands to his shoulders and held her hips as he continued backing deeper into the lake. Her fingernails dug into his skin when the ground sloped so she couldn't touch.

"I've got you," he promised. "Just start moving your legs back and forth."

Her lips curved into a smile as she followed his instructions. "Oh."

Torin paused to allow her time to get used to moving in the water. Then he began walking backwards again. He didn't tell her when it became too deep for him. She looked between him and the shoreline.

"I've got you. Now, move your arms back and forth as you kick your legs."

She paused for a heartbeat before she released his shoulders and once more followed his guidance. Her smile grew as she mastered the technique. Torin knew he could've let go of her because she was treading water, but he didn't.

"Look down," he urged.

She dipped her chin and gasped when a school of brightly colored fish swam beneath them. Her head snapped up. "You aren't touching the ground?"

"Haven't been in a while."

More fish caught her attention. "Look at all of them."

"Want to see them better?"

She hesitated, then nodded. He grinned and caught her hands in his. She held her mouth tightly as her anxiety rose.

"I won't let go. You tell me where you want to turn, and I'll turn you."

Breda nodded and refocused on the water. "The water is so clear."

"The depth is deceptive."

"Surely, it isn't that far."

Torin grinned. "It's farther than you think."

"Show me."

He was shocked at her statement. "I won't be long."

"No," she said and gripped his hands tighter. "Take me down with you."

His brows rose as she surprised him again. "Are you sure?"

"Like you said, I can do magic. I won't drown."

"Watch what I do. If it becomes too much, squeeze my hand, and I'll get us to shore immediately."

The fear ebbed from her face as she nodded. That's when it struck him that she trusted him. Completely. After everything she had been through, after everything she had suffered, she lowered her barriers and let him in. Without a doubt, she had borne more than he, and yet, she didn't hold onto it as he had—as all the Reapers did.

She had been betrayed, multiple times. She was manipulated. People had lied to her. And yet, here she was, wearing a soft smile and giving him her trust. It humbled him. Affected him deeply that she would grant him such a gift.

Because it *was* a gift.

"Really?" he asked.

She nodded once. "It's not a big deal."

"It is."

"Maybe a little."

He quirked a brow. "A lot."

"You seem surprised."

"Aye. And honored."

It was her turn to give a shocked look. "Am I scared of the Others? Yes. Am I scared of the Reapers and Death? Yes. Am I scared of you?" She gazed at him for a long moment then softly said, "No. You've repeatedly shown me that I can trust you."

"What if I betray you?"

"Then you do. Me worrying about it won't stop it from happening. Nor will anything I say or do."

He twisted his lips. "I disagree with that. If you don't trust people, they can't betray you."

"That's true to a degree. But I can't live my life in a shell. There's so much more to experience."

"I'm envious that you've found that kind of contentment."

She grinned, her crimson eyes crinkling. "Odd since you're the one who has shown me that path."

"What?" he asked in astonishment.

"You've pushed me to see more, learn more. You've protected me. Made me feel protected for the first time in my life. You've shown me that despite your past, you found a group where you belong. I'm the one who is envious of you."

He pulled her against him and gazed into her eyes. "I think we've been good for each other."

"I couldn't agree more," she said as she gently touched his face.

Torin lowered his head and kissed her. His body burned to sink inside her tight, wet heat. The desire ran hot as lava through his veins, but more than that, he felt the connection between them. He'd sensed it the first time he'd seen her. And the more he got to know her, the more they talked, the more it grew until it became a solid, firm entity.

Breda ended the kiss and smiled. "Take me below the water."

"Remember," he said as he took her hand, "squeeze if it becomes too much."

"I will."

"Use your magic to breathe under the water."

She kept her gaze locked with his, following his every movement. After their magic was in place, he dove beneath the surface, taking her with him. Torin glanced at her to see her eyes open and smiling. She pointed to this fish and that. Her amazement and pleasure made him smile, too.

About halfway down, he expected her to want to return to the surface, but she surprised him yet again. The courage and tenacity she had shown when climbing the mountain soon kicked in. She didn't let go of his hand, but she used her other arm and legs to propel herself forward, mimicking his movements. The closer to the bottom they got, the more confident she became. He let her choose which direction to go as they explored the lakebed and the various aquatic life.

Nearly an hour later, she finally pointed upward and tugged her hand from his. He nodded and remained near her as she swam alone to the surface. When his head broke the water, he heard her let out the same kind of elated shout that she had upon climbing the mountain. It made him wonder what things he could've done had he embraced life with such enthusiasm and joy.

"That was incredible," she said, her face alight with happiness. "Thank you."

"My pleasure."

She gave him a dignified smile. "I'm treading water, if you hadn't noticed."

"I noticed," he said with a laugh.

"I was so scared for so long to even get into the water. I can't believe I didn't try this sooner."

Breda proved once more that she was something special. "Do you want to swim to shore?"

She glanced to where she had slept earlier. "Uh…I don't think that's an option."

Torin followed her gaze and spotted Balladyn. Without a word to Breda, he grabbed her, teleporting them to shore. They arrived dry and clothed.

"What is it?" Torin asked Balladyn.

The former King met his gaze. "I'm sorry to interrupt. Eoghan is here."

Torin glanced at Breda. "We can return later."

"I understand. Other matters need to be addressed," she said.

Torin looked at the water. The few hours they'd shared had been life-altering in many ways. He might have given his vow to Breda to get information, but now, he would protect her at all costs. From any foe.

"Let's go," he said and held out his hand for her.

Balladyn vanished a heartbeat before Breda's palm slid into his. In the next second, Torin jumped them outside the tent. Eoghan stood at the entrance. His gaze lingered on Torin for a moment before his quicksilver eyes slid to Breda.

"You've come for more information," she said.

Eoghan bowed his head in acknowledgement. "Time is of the essence."

"I know that more than most," Breda said and entered the tent when Eoghan held it open.

When Torin started to follow, Eoghan stepped in his way. Torin pulled up and met his leader's gaze.

"You look different," Eoghan stated.

Torin thought about his morning with Breda. "Because I am."

"I take it our guest is the reason?"

"We never speak of our pasts, of why we became Reapers. You know ours because you lead us and need to know why we react the way we do."

Eoghan nodded. "That's right."

"I might not have let it show, but anger ruled me. In every decision. I couldn't let go of the betrayal that made me a Reaper."

There was a slight smile to Eoghan's lips. "You didn't hide it as well as you thought."

Torin chuckled. "I guess I didn't."

"What of the anger now?"

"It's still there, but it's faded to the background. I can't forget it happened, but…"

"You're ready to move on." Eoghan pressed his lips together. "I remember the day that happened to me. It was a profound moment. Enjoy it."

Torin drew in a deep breath, feeling lighter and freer than ever before. "I intend to."

CHAPTER SIXTEEN

When the tent entrance fell closed behind her without Eoghan or Torin following, Breda turned to look at it. She couldn't help but wonder why they hadn't come in.

"You've got a nice glow from the sun."

Breda's head turned toward the sofa at the sound of Balladyn's voice. She found him sitting in the middle of the U-shaped couch with his ankles crossed and his feet resting on the table.

"Were we away too long?" she asked as she walked to the sofa and took the same side as she had the previous night.

Balladyn laced his fingers together behind his head. "Torin isn't in trouble, if that's what you're wondering."

She twisted her lips and glanced at the entrance. "Are you sure?"

"Positive," he said with a smile. "No kidding, though. The glow looks good on you."

Breda smiled at the compliment. "Thanks."

"Though I don't think the sun is the only thing making you beam."

She pressed her lips together and swallowed. "The sun definitely played a part, but you're right, it isn't the only thing."

Balladyn's smile was slow as it grew. He shot her a wink. "Good for you both."

Breda wanted to be happy, but worry was beginning to set in. "What if I don't give enough information on the Others? What happens to me?"

"You'll be protected. That, I can assure you. Just tell us everything you know. You've already shared a lot, which confirms things we already knew."

Before she could reply, someone pulled the fabric at the entrance aside, and Eoghan straightened after ducking to enter, followed immediately by Torin. She held Torin's gaze for a moment and then looked at Eoghan. The tall Light Fae with the quicksilver eyes took the cushion opposite her. She wanted to know why Eoghan's eyes were so different, but she told herself that now wasn't the time to ask.

"We weren't properly introduced earlier," Eoghan said with an easy smile. "I'm Eoghan."

Breda opened her mouth to say that she was glad to meet him, but what came out was, "Why are your eyes different?" The instant she realized what she had done, she cringed. "I'm sorry. I have a horrible habit of allowing my curiosity to get the better of me."

Eoghan chuckled and rested his arm along the back of the sofa. "When we were fighting an enemy, I took a blow of magic meant for someone else. It threw me to another realm that was…anything but hospitable. When I found my way back to Earth, my eyes looked like this."

"They're beautiful," she said in awe. "Do you see differently?"

"Not at all. I wouldn't have known they'd changed if my friends hadn't alerted me."

Breda tucked one foot beneath her and clasped her hands in her lap. "Thank you for indulging me. It's nice to meet you, Eoghan. I've been astonished and completely taken in by all of you."

"Because of what you learned through the Others?" he asked.

She nodded, glancing at Torin, who remained by the entrance, his feet set in a wide stance, his arms crossed over his chest. "I didn't believe any stories I heard about the Reapers as a child, so to be told that you were real came as quite a shock."

"So, you heard the normal stories Fae children are told?" Eoghan asked.

Breda hesitated and looked at Torin. He gave her a slow nod. It had been difficult to tell him. She didn't want to repeat the story, but Eoghan and the others needed a complete picture of her life and the part the Others played in it.

She drew in a shaky breath and retold her story to Eoghan and Balladyn but kept her gaze on the table. Oddly, the second time was easier than the first. When she finished and looked up, Eoghan had a peculiar look on his face. Balladyn had lowered his arms to his lap. It wasn't pity she saw on either of their faces, but kindness and understanding.

"You're an incredibly strong individual to have survived all of that and be standing here today," Eoghan said.

Balladyn added, "With a smile, no less."

"Precisely." Eoghan scratched his neck. "The fact that you have three-quarters Fae blood is why you so easily moved through our world. I'm sure I don't have to tell you what could've happened had anyone discovered the truth."

Breda shrugged. "There are Halflings everywhere."

"Not in our world," Balladyn said.

"It's okay to leave them with humans, but they can't remain with the Fae?" She scrunched her face. "That's racism."

Eoghan blew out a breath. "It's the way it's always been."

"Why?" she pressed. "If mortals are good enough to have sex with, why shouldn't a female Fae keep her child?"

Balladyn lowered his feet to the floor. "Because the Fae know that the Halfling would never survive in our world. They would be bullied for being unable to do the magic that comes naturally to a full-blooded Fae."

"You don't think Halflings get bullied in the mortal world?"

Torin said, "That isn't what Balladyn is saying. As much as humans and Fae look similar, our genetic makeup is different."

She eyed all three men. "Halflings don't fit into either world.

They're left to fend for themselves. Some have families, but most of those families have no idea what to do with a Halfling that exhibits behaviors they don't understand."

"You make a good point," Balladyn said. "I realize you speak from some experience, but even you have more Fae blood than a Halfling. When a female becomes pregnant by a human in our culture, many decide to have an abortion. Others usually leave the infant with the father after giving birth. I've never heard of a Fae— Light or Dark—who has kept the babe to raise."

Breda was learning things she hadn't dared to ask other Fae before for fear of bringing too much attention to herself.

"You never spoke of your father," Torin said.

"I never found out his name. I only knew about him being a Halfling because Mum liked to throw it in my face."

Eoghan cleared his throat and glanced at the ground. "Was he your siblings' father, as well?"

"Mum hated everyone and everything. She sought solace in alcohol and sex. None of her children had the same father," Breda explained.

Balladyn caught her gaze. "We can't pick our parents. Don't carry shame for her decisions."

Breda gave him a grateful smile. He was right. She shouldn't feel embarrassed about her mum's decisions and actions. That was on her mother. With that realization, she cut one of the cords tying her to her old life.

"Is your family still alive?" Eoghan asked.

Breda glanced at the ground. "Yes."

"Then they could turn on you to the Others," Torin replied.

She met his gaze and nodded.

Balladyn grunted. "We need to see about that."

"Agreed. Breda, Torin said you could describe the Others," Eoghan said.

She nodded eagerly. "The Six, yes. They never said names, but I saw their faces often enough. Three Dark, three Light. Only one male, and he was Dark."

"Was he the leader?" Balladyn asked.

Breda shook her head. "The one who led the meetings was a Light. I don't know if she's the leader, but it appeared that way."

"Give me every detail," Eoghan said.

Torin grunted. "They could've used glamour to hide their true faces."

"They didn't," Balladyn said.

Breda frowned. "How can you be sure?"

"They're driven by their inflated egos," he stated evenly.

Eoghan ran a hand over his jaw. "It would take Fae with very high opinions of themselves to step into such roles."

"As well as being powerful," Torin added.

Breda glanced at the three of them. "Or pretending to be, like I was."

"There are two possibilities," Balladyn explained. "They either truly believe they're doing the right thing—in which case they don't see themselves as anything but saviors."

Torin shook his head. "Or, they're so power-hungry, they don't care who gets destroyed on their way to the top."

"If it's the latter, it's only a matter of time before they turn on each other," Eoghan said.

Balladyn lifted one shoulder in a shrug. "We can't wait to find out."

All eyes turned to her then. "Descriptions?" she asked.

"Descriptions," Eoghan said.

Breda licked her lips and closed her eyes, picturing the last meeting. "The Light female who appears to be the leader is tall. She has a pixie hairstyle that accentuates her long neck. She speaks as if she's cultured, but sometimes it appears as if she has to remind herself of that fact."

"As if it doesn't come naturally?" Balladyn asked.

Breda opened her eyes and nodded to the Dark. "Exactly. Like she knows how to speak that way, but it isn't something she's done for most of her life."

"That's good. That helps a lot," Eoghan said. "What else?"

Breda closed her eyes again. "She likes to be the focus. It's in the way she smiles when she's talking and knows everyone is looking at her. To her right is another Light. This woman is several inches shorter and beginning to show some signs of aging, but still incredibly beautiful and elegant. I've always thought she wears age like a badge. Like it's important for everyone to know that she has lived a long life and experienced things. She thinks before she speaks, considering her words carefully. She has a way about her that speaks of nobility, and with her, it comes naturally. Her hair is always up and contained in some style, so I don't know the exact length. The third Light is on the leader's left. You can tell she's used to getting what she wants. She's poised but discerning. Her hair is long, and she spends time coiffing it to bring attention to the luxurious onyx strands. She isn't as careful with her words. She's quick to speak and react.

"The Dark male stands in the middle of the two Dark females. It's difficult to determine his age, but he has an anger about him that is difficult to miss. His hair is different each time he comes, but there is more silver than black in it. To others, he might seem to be outnumbered, but he shouldn't be underestimated. He's someone to worry about. The Dark female to his left is usual height and has medium-length hair and two thick strands of silver on each side of her head. She constantly eyes the others as if waiting for her chance to do something extraordinary. The Dark female on the male's right is petite and waif-thin. She rarely has any emotion on her face, but her eyes can cut sharper than a blade. She keeps her black and silver hair in a ponytail as if the thought of styling it is too much. She's sees everything."

After a moment, Breda opened her eyes when silence met her words. She found the three men staring at her.

"With your descriptions, we should be able to pick them out even if they use glamour," Torin said.

Balladyn nodded when she looked at him. "That was impressive. You picked out details others might have missed while trying to describe faces."

"Well done," Eoghan told her.

Breda's shoulders dropped as she smiled at the three. Maybe there was a chance of finding the Six before they found the Reapers.

CHAPTER SEVENTEEN

Torin was sure that with the descriptions Breda had given them, they would be able to find at least one of the Six. When Eoghan asked her the same questions Torin and Aisling had, Breda didn't object. For the next two hours, she answered each with as much conviction and diligence as she had with her verbal depictions.

Finally, Eoghan relented and turned his attention to Balladyn. "Is there any chance one of the Dark Breda described sounds familiar?"

"You've been in the Dark Palace. What do you think?" Balladyn answered.

Eoghan grunted and leaned back against the cushions. "That's what I thought."

"What now?" Breda asked as she looked from Eoghan to Torin.

"Now, we hunt," Balladyn replied.

Torin smiled at Balladyn before turning his gaze to Eoghan. He wanted to go after the Others and stop them before they wreaked havoc upon the realm. His thoughts halted when he thought of Breda. He looked her way to find her staring at him.

"I'll be fine here," she said.

He shook his head. "No."

"Torin's right," Eoghan said before Breda could respond. "The information you have is too valuable. You've imparted quite a bit, and there may still be more you've not thought of. I'm not willing to chance the soldiers finding you, and I know Erith feels the same."

Breda got to her feet and calmly told Eoghan, "You're going to need all the Reapers. That means Torin, too. Aisling is gone, so you're already down one. You can't afford to leave anyone behind."

"She has a point," Balladyn said.

Torin crossed his arms over his chest. "Breda isn't being left alone."

"Maybe she doesn't need to be," Eoghan said.

It took but a second for Torin to get what his leader implied. The thought terrified him. "No."

"What?" Breda asked as she looked between the three of them.

Torin and Eoghan stared at each other. Torin wasn't backing down. It was the first time he had stood against Eoghan, and he would accept whatever consequences occurred because of it.

"Eoghan wants to use you as bait," Balladyn told her.

Torin's head snapped to Balladyn. "What the fek?"

"Yes," Breda replied with a nod as her crimson eyes found his. "Think about it. It's perfect. You won't have to waste time hunting. They'll come for me."

Torin dropped his hands and turned away to pace a few steps before he spun back around. "It won't be the Six who come. It'll be the soldiers."

"Who will take me to the Six."

He was so taken aback by her comment that he was at a loss for words for a second. "Have you lost your mind? Not only do you want the soldiers to find you, but you also want to be taken to the Six?"

"Yes," she replied succinctly.

Balladyn blew out a breath. "That's a bold and risky move."

"It's fekking ridiculous," Torin barked.

Eoghan slowly released a breath. "It could work. We'll stay veiled and follow them."

Torin was so angry, he wanted to shout. "Need I remind all of

you that the soldiers know to send out magic to reveal anyone who is
veiled?"

"We could find a solution," Eoghan said.

Torin raked a hand through his hair as he started pacing
again. No one seemed to understand how dangerous this endeavor
was.

"It's ultimately my decision," Breda said.

That drew him up short. He looked into her eyes and shook his
head. "What you're proposing is tantamount to suicide."

"Not if you're there. Besides, the Others need to be taken
down."

"We can find another way."

She smiled as she walked to him. "They want me. They want to
make an example of me. If you can come up with another way to
find them, then I'm all ears. But," she said as she glanced at
Eoghan, "if you had another option, it would have already been put
into place."

"Fek!" Torin said as he glared first at Breda and then Eoghan.

Torin's wrath didn't daunt Eoghan. "I'll return shortly."

No sooner had Eoghan teleported out than Balladyn got to his
feet and walked from the tent without a word.

"If you were able, would you do it?"

Torin looked down at Breda. He didn't pretend not to know
what she was asking. "It's different."

"It isn't," she said with a shake of her head.

"I'm a warrior. I know what I'd be getting into."

She put a foot out and cocked a hip as she crossed her arms over
her chest. "Oh, really? And you've been to the meetings? You've
seen what is done to those who try to leave?"

"You know I haven't."

"Exactly. I have."

"Which is all the more reason you shouldn't go."

Breda dropped her arms and moved the last two steps to reach
him. She put her hands on his chest and moved them up to wind
around his neck. "It's the very reason I *have* to go. I'm the only one
who can bring you to the Six."

"*You* won't be doing a bloody thing. You'll be a prisoner," he pointed out.

"You're a Reaper. You can do things I don't begin to know. If you can remain veiled and follow me to the Others, then there's your way in. You can stop them once and for all."

He sighed as he wrapped his arms around her. "What happens if we lose you? Have you thought of that?"

"You won't let that happen."

"You're damn right, I won't," he stated.

She smiled. "I've existed so long in fear. You've shown me how to live, and for the first time, I can do something good. I'm useful. Let me do this to stop the innocent Fae from being killed because the Six didn't accept them into the organization. Let me be the bait so you and the other Reapers can end the Others."

"I'm not sure I can."

"You might think it's a death sentence, but I'm willing to do this because I know you'll be there. You gave me your vow to keep me safe. I expect you to keep it."

Torin pulled her against him and simply held her. He had never been in such a position before. He cared for Breda. Deeply. More than he had felt for any other being. She had healed parts of him he hadn't realized were wounded. If he could feel that way after such a short time, what would his life be like if she were by his side for eternity?

He knew that's exactly where he wanted her. The Reapers were powerful, and they had a goddess on their side, but the Six and their soldiers were an unknown variable. There was no guarantee that the additional power the Reapers received from Erith would be enough to win against them. Which meant Breda could be killed.

Just thinking about it made Torin's chest constrict like a band of steel tightening around him. Breda had pushed aside the darkness that hung over him. She had allowed him to release the past and step into the sunlight. How could he willingly help her make a decision that had the potential to take away the very thing he now craved with all of his being?

Torin released her and strode from the tent. He needed air and time to think. Being around Breda confused him even more because he didn't want to put her in danger, even though he knew the plan was one he would usually be behind. There was a way for the Reapers to find the Others and keep Breda safe. He just had to find the answer.

He walked aimlessly, his mind moving, replaying everything that had happened within the tent. He came at the problem several different ways, and each time it left him as annoyed as when he'd begun. The simple fact was they needed to stop the Others before they killed more Fae. If the Six gained more power, more than the Fae were in danger.

The Dragon Kings would step in and protect the realm as they always had, but would it be enough? Would the Six have enough power to overtake them? Torin wasn't sure they could, but he didn't want to bet everything on the Kings. This was a Fae problem, and it needed to be dealt with by the Reapers and Erith.

Death could usually find any Fae she sought, but she hadn't been able to locate Usaeil when they had looked for her. Erith hadn't been able to locate Xaneth when Usaeil had held him prisoner, and Death hadn't been able to find the Fae Others. If Erith couldn't uncover them, then that left only one option: use Breda as bait.

Yet the very thought repulsed Torin.

"You realize the decision is out of your hands, right?"

Torin spun around at the sound of Balladyn's voice. "There's another way."

"There isn't. And you know it."

"I can't let her do this."

"You're not *letting* her do anything. If you think that, you're a fool. And you aren't a fool."

Torin turned his head to the side. "This morning began as the best day I've ever had. Now, it's ending as the worst."

"Don't let it."

Torin returned his gaze to Balladyn. "Meaning?"

"We're Reapers. Breda is putting her life in our hands because she knows we'll protect her. I'm betting she said as much to you.

She's going to use herself as bait. Now, you can remain here trying to find a way to stop that from happening, or you can go back to her and end the day as you began it—with her."

Torin glanced at the tent. "I think...I think I'm falling in love with her."

"You sound surprised," Balladyn said with a smile.

"I didn't want to love."

Balladyn shrugged. "We don't get a say in things like that."

"What will happen if I lose her?"

"Perhaps you should think about what can happen if you don't."

Torin flashed him a smile. "I don't know if I ever told you, but I'm sorry your reign got cut short."

"I'm where I'm supposed to be." He jerked his head toward the tent. "Now, why don't you get where you're supposed to be."

Torin slapped him on the arm as he hurried past. He rushed into the tent, but Breda wasn't in the common area. His gaze moved to the room she had chosen. The fabric was closed, telling him she was inside.

He walked to stand before it and moved the curtain aside with his hand to peer inside. Breda lay on her side on the bed without any clothes. Torin's eyes lingered on the silhouette of her body, his cock thickening at the sight of her. His eyes lowered to her full breasts to see that her nipples were hard.

"About time," she said with a seductive smile.

Torin stepped inside the room and let the curtain fall closed behind him. She rose on her knees and held out a hand. He took it and let her pull him close. His legs bumped against the side of the bed as she gazed into his eyes.

He rested his hands on her shoulders and caressed down her sides to the indent of her waist and over her hips before cupping her butt and grinding against her so she could feel his arousal.

"Mmm. Promise we won't be interrupted," she murmured while placing light kisses on his lips.

"I promise."

Her smile was luminescent. "Just what I wanted to hear."

He lowered his head for a kiss, but she slipped out of his arms and off the bed. He turned to find her behind him. She locked her eyes on him and dropped to her knees. His cock jumped in response. With a thought, his clothes were gone.

She winked at him. Then she reached for him, wrapping her fingers around his length and moving her hand up and down. His eyes closed at the pleasure while her other hand cupped his sac and massaged his balls.

A groan left him when her lips wrapped around him. Torin looked down to see her bobbing her head on his cock. It wouldn't take much for him to finish. Just the sight of her mouth on him was enough for him to climax.

But he had other ideas.

CHAPTER EIGHTEEN

A surprised gasp left Breda when she found herself on her back on the bed with Torin on his knees on the floor. He parted her legs and flashed her a smile before licking her. She sighed and dropped her head back.

His skilled tongue teased her clit, effortlessly building her desire until she gripped the blanket with both hands. She cried out with pleasure when he reached up and rolled her nipple between two of his fingers.

No one built a fire inside her like Torin. No one had ever touched her so exquisitely, so perfectly. And no one had ever brought her such mindboggling pleasure.

She felt the orgasm building too quickly. She tried to pull away, but he held her hips firmly in place with both hands, refusing to let her escape. Breda attempted to use her voice, but it was too late. The pleasure built rapidly with each twirl of his tongue. She was powerless to resist the lure of ecstasy she knew awaited her. Breda reached for it, eager for the climax.

When it struck, she arched her back, her body pulsing. Torin's tongue continued its beautiful torture, extending her orgasm to the point where her body became a quivering mass.

"P-please." She begged for him to stop.

The pleasure was so intense, so powerful that she couldn't catch her breath. He took pity on her and granted her plea. But the reprieve was quick. He flipped her onto her stomach and lifted her hips. She glanced over her shoulder to see Torin guiding his cock to her entrance. Their gazes met as he slid inside her. The satisfaction on his face heightened her desire to a whole new level.

Her sex clenched around him, causing him to moan. She repeated the movement a second time. But if she thought to get the upper hand and make him as weak-kneed as she was, she was sorely mistaken.

Torin reached around and found her swollen, sensitive clit, circling it with a finger. She gasped at the sensations that rushed through her. He pumped his hips in long, slow thrusts. The feel of his length moving inside her was everything she needed. His warm breath fanned her ear, his breaths as erratic as hers.

He straightened behind her and grabbed her hips as he quickened his rhythm. The sound of his balls slapping against her made her sex throb in anticipation.

Desire thrummed hotly through Torin. He had nearly come at the sight of Breda's orgasm. It was by sheer will alone that he had held back. After her mouth on his cock, and then watching the pleasure move over her body, he walked a fine line.

Their union that morning had been quick and passionate. He wanted this time to go slower, but one look at her, and nothing mattered but the shared pleasure he knew awaited.

He gazed at her back, her soft skin dewy with sweat. Her moans were low and seductive, her wet heat pushing him ever closer to coming. When she leaned back against him whenever he thrust, he sank deeper into her.

She moaned, making his blood quicken.

His fingers dug into her hips as he drove deeper, harder.

"Torin," she called in a strangled voice, letting him know that she was close to climaxing.

He gritted his teeth, pushing them both to the very edge. "Now!" he shouted as he succumbed to his orgasm.

The feel of her body clutching around his cock made him gasp with pleasure. He lost track of time, forgot everything but Breda and the rapture that had overtaken them. When he came back to the present, his body shook from the force of their joining.

Torin gently pulled out of her and rolled onto his back. She collapsed, her face turned to him. They shared a smile before he pulled her against him. He'd been eager for battles and danger for so long. Now, all he wanted was Breda and peace. That wouldn't come until the Others were gone.

In order to rid his people of the Others, the Reapers had to find them. Which brought him back to *how*. Even if they did find the Others, how could the Reapers and Death ensure that no one else banded together and tried the same thing?

The original group of Others had kept their faction secret. These Fae were the opposite. They wanted everyone to know of their existence. Unless the Fae came to the conclusion that the Others were wrong and forming another unit was senseless, he and the Reapers would be in a constant loop of taking down group after group.

There was one way they could do that, but it would involve something rash and potentially hazardous. And not just to the Reapers, but to Erith herself.

"I'd like to think your thoughts are on the pleasure we just shared," Breda said, breaking into his thoughts. "But by the frown on your face, I gather you're thinking about the Others."

He sighed and tightened his arm around her. "There's another answer out there that doesn't involve you offering yourself up as bait."

Breda blew out a breath and moved to straddle his hips. "I don't want to think about that right now. I don't want to talk about that right now." Her lips curved into a smile that was both seductive and sly.

"Oh?" Torin asked.

"I have something better in mind," she replied before rising onto her knees and taking hold of his cock.

Her hands were masterful in their touch. He was hard in seconds. Just as she wanted, the only thing on his mind was Breda as she lowered herself.

Balladyn tossed a stone into the river as his thoughts drifted. The Others never should've been in existence to begin with. They wouldn't have, had Usaeil not joined. For millions of years, the Others had been so secret that no one had known about them—or their goal to rid the Earth of the Dragon Kings.

He'd been King of the Dark then and had joined with the Reapers and Dragon Kings to take down Usaeil once and for all. The Dark had answered his call and fought alongside the Light in an epic showdown.

It should've been over then.

It had been over.

Yet the Fae and Druids had begun their own groups. There was something at work here. Something that moved just under the radar. Three of the six original members of the Others were confirmed dead. The Fae, Brian, was still left unaccounted for. That left the two human Druids. It made sense that they would rile up the Druids, but the Fae? What was he missing? Could it be Brian? Had they all made a mistake in letting him go because they believed he was a coward?

"You look deep in thought," Eoghan said as he walked up.

Balladyn glanced at him. "You returned quick."

"Is Torin still upset?"

"He and Breda are in the tent."

Eoghan glanced at the structure. "Ah. I see. Let's leave them for the night, then."

"My thoughts exactly."

"What's going on in that brain of yours?"

Balladyn returned his gaze to the flowing water of the river. "Wondering how the new Others came into being."

"You aren't the only one."

His head turned back to Eoghan. "And? Do you know something?"

"Not yet."

"It should be our focus," he snapped.

Eoghan didn't react to the anger. "Erith is only one goddess. She still has her duties to keep the balance within the Fae. Not to mention, she hasn't given up on finding Xaneth. On top of both of those things are the Six, their soldiers, the thousands of Fae being killed in the Others' name, all while worrying that the group just might locate us."

Balladyn let out a long sigh. He knew better than most what it felt like to be in a position of power and the heavy weight it entailed. "My apologies."

"There's no need," he began.

"There is, actually. I just feel…" He shrugged, unable to find the word.

Eoghan's lips flattened. "Helpless? Powerless? Aching to do *some*thing other than sit and wait?"

Balladyn nodded. "All of those things."

"We are all experiencing that. The Reapers have remained hidden since our inception. The Others have shifted things. We're no longer scary tales told to young Fae. Our people are actively looking for us. I'm thankful now, more than ever, that we live on Erith's realm instead of Earth."

"Whoever is leading the Others is knowledgeable enough to know about us and understand we're powerful. They want us taken out first."

Eoghan nodded slowly. "Breda told Torin and Aisling that one of the Others had seen us. We need to determine when that happened."

Balladyn tossed another pebble into the air and caught it with his hand before swinging his arm back and letting the rock fly to skip across the water several times before disappearing. "My vote is the Light leading them."

"Why do you think that?"

He looked at Eoghan and grinned. "Because she's running things. Breda said she wasn't sure who was in charge, but if the female Light always controlled the meetings, then she's in charge."

"That doesn't mean she's the one who saw us," Eoghan said with a frown. "Determining who saw us and where will be tricky."

"Why does it matter?"

"If we know where the Fae was, we'll know what they saw."

Balladyn scrunched up his face. "The fact is, someone saw something. They aren't the first one, either. Kyra saw us."

"Don't remind me," Eoghan said with a sigh. He put his hands on his hips and shook his head. "We've always been so careful."

"That doesn't matter anymore. There have always been Fae who believed the Reapers were real. I did, before I knew for certain. There was mention of you in books."

Eoghan's quicksilver eyes met his. "Rumors have always swirled. This is much more than rumors."

"Like it or not, things have changed. We need to react instead of sitting by and waiting for something to happen."

"My thoughts exactly," said a female voice behind him.

Balladyn looked over his shoulder to find none other than Death and her consort, Cael.

CHAPTER NINETEEN

The sound of Torin's heart beating soothed Breda from where she sat between his legs, resting against his chest. He had his arms wrapped around her, holding her loosely as her fingers idly drew designs on his hands and forearms. The night had gone by too fast. For the last hour, they had been in this position, simply enjoying being with each other.

Torin's arm rose to wrap around the front of her shoulders as he pressed his lips to her temple. "I wish I could stop time."

"We'll be back."

He situated his head next to hers. "I didn't take you for an optimist."

She chuckled and glanced at him before giving him a quick kiss. "I'm putting a positive spin on this. Think confidently, then it'll happen."

"There's nothing I can do to change your mind, is there?"

They hadn't spoken about her plan to hand herself over to the soldiers since he'd come into her room. She had hoped they wouldn't discuss it at all, but that had been too much to wish for. "If you were in my position, you wouldn't hesitate to do it."

"That doesn't mean I have to like it."

"They need to be stopped. It's a fact. We can stay here and spend eternity in each other's arms. I'd like nothing better. But I'd never forgive myself, knowing that I had a chance to stop the slaughter of innocent Fae yet didn't do anything."

He grunted. "Not all of them are innocent."

"They're still being murdered. No one deserves that." She wrinkled her nose. "Well, there might be a few, but that isn't for us to decide."

Torin turned her so that she faced him. His finger slid from her forehead to her ear, moving a strand of hair from her face. He smiled, his silver eyes locked with hers. "Something happened to me here."

"It happened to me, too," she said with a grin. "So many times, I lost count."

He chuckled. "That's not what I meant."

Her smile died with her shrug. "I know."

"I'm scared that if you go, you won't return."

She had done her best to shield her heart from Torin, but his tender touch, passionate loving, and heartfelt words had busted through her walls. Breda cupped his face with her hand and smiled through the strong feelings swirling inside her. "I might not. I'm going to do everything I can to return, but it might be out of our control."

"I love you."

No one had ever said those words to her before. They meant more than he could ever know. Her throat clogged with emotion so thick, she couldn't find her voice. Tears threatened, but she refused to let them flow. She had to be strong. Otherwise, she would cave and not use herself as bait. She talked a good game, but she was terrified.

Being with Torin was indescribable. He knew her secrets and had earned her trust as no one else had. He protected her while also pushing her. She had grown more in the short time she had been with him than in her entire life. It was impossible to give up what she had found.

But she had no choice.

She was the way in, what the Reapers needed to get to the Others. Breda hoped that she didn't end up dead, but she was a realist. She understood the odds, and though she hated it, she accepted them. The only way she could do that was by keeping her feelings to herself.

"You taught me to swim," she said with a smile.

He took her hand and kissed the middle of her palm. "I didn't teach you. I simply showed you what you could do."

"I don't suppose you want to try to attempt to stop time, do you? I'm not ready to leave."

"Then don't."

She glanced at their joined hands. "I can only do this if you're with me."

"I'll be by your side the entire time," he stated fervently.

Breda leaned forward and placed her hands on either side of his head as she pressed her lips against his. He yanked her against him, shifting so he stretched out and she lay on top of him. He rolled her onto her back and deepened the kiss. His hand skimmed down her body and between her legs.

"Breda. Torin," Eoghan called.

Torin ended the kiss and pressed his forehead to hers. "Our time is up."

"For now," she reminded him with a smile.

His lips curved slightly as he rolled away from her and got to his feet. "We're coming," he told Eoghan. Torin turned to her. "One last chance."

It was more tempting than he knew. Somehow, she managed to shake her head. His disappointment was clear as clothes suddenly appeared on his body. He didn't wait for her as he moved aside the curtain and stepped out.

Breda sat up and drew her legs to her chest. She tucked her chin, resting her forehead on her knees as she gave in to the wave of tears. It was so unfair to finally find a semblance of happiness only to lose it. Because while she talked about being positive in the outcome of going to the Others, it was all malarkey—her attempt to be brave.

She lifted her head and sniffed. The other truth she hadn't allowed herself to think about was that she likely wouldn't be able to stay with Torin regardless. She would be relegated to the Fae Realm, and he had duties with the Reapers. They would likely spend more time apart than together. If they were able to be with each other.

While he had told her a good bit about the Reapers, they hadn't talked about relationships. The Reapers she had seen had been alone, but that didn't mean anything. Or it could mean exactly that.

She pressed the heels of her hands to her temples as her head began to throb. If she continued down this train of thought, she would be such a bundle of nerves that she would never go through with offering herself up as bait. She had to forget about Torin's confession of love and yearning to find true happiness and pull herself together.

Breda swiped at the tears and climbed off the bed. If she were going to do this, then she would look the part. She opted for her favorite biker boots, dark denim, an olive-green tank top with Princess Leia that said, *Don't call me princess* that she paired with a black leather biker jacket. She swiped her hair over to her left side and released a breath. After she squared her shoulders, she walked into the common area, only to find it empty.

She exited the tent and found Torin, Eoghan, and Balladyn standing together in the morning sun. Torin noticed her first. He stopped mid-sentence. The other two turned their heads to her. No one moved. She kept her head high as she walked to them.

"Eoghan," she acknowledged.

He gazed at her for a long moment. "Are you still sure about this?"

"I wish everyone would stop asking me that." It came out harsher than intended because she was scared.

Balladyn crossed his arms over his chest. "We're inquiring to make sure you haven't changed your mind."

"Which you can do," Torin said.

Eoghan nodded. "Absolutely."

"Thank you," she told them. "I appreciate all of this, but I'm going through with it."

"Do you have combat training?" Balladyn asked.

Breda cut her eyes to him and shook her head. "I'm not completely without skills, but I'm sure it's nothing like what you can do."

"We'll be there to help," Torin stated.

Eoghan glanced at him. "Aye, we will be."

"It's fine," Breda said told him. "Your first priority is to the Reapers."

"Don't think we're taking what you're doing lightly," Eoghan replied.

Breda felt Torin's eyes on her. She desperately wanted to go to him and have his arms around her. To leave the first place she had been safe, with the first person who had ever truly cared about her would be the toughest thing she had ever done.

"Are we doing this now?" she asked.

Balladyn lifted one shoulder. "The sooner, the better."

"My thoughts exactly," Breda said before Torin could speak.

Eoghan cleared his throat. "There's someone here who would like to speak with you."

A chill went up Breda's spin. She knew without turning around that someone was behind her. She met Torin's gaze. He gave her a small nod of encouragement. She turned to find a man and a woman standing between her and the tent. The man was tall with long, coal-black hair. She would've pegged him as a Fae, but his eyes were purple. He stood with a slight smile as he met her gaze.

The woman was petite, barely reaching the man's shoulder, and gorgeous. She had very long, wavy, blue-black hair, pulled back on the sides. Large, lavender eyes watched her peculiarly. The woman wore a sexy, badass, all-black ensemble that consisted of a sleeveless brocade corset with leather sides and a sweetheart neckline, leather pants, and a low-slung belt and boots.

The instant Breda saw Aisling, she'd known the Reaper was a warrior. The woman before her had that same edge, along with a timelessness that defied words. That's how Breda knew she was standing before Death.

"You're very eager to face the Others," the male said.

Breda slid her gaze to him. "Don't mistake my willingness to be bait for wanting to be near any of them again. I'm doing this because I'm the only one who can. And because I can't live knowing that Fae are being slaughtered."

"Some might think the Fae need to be thinned out," the woman replied.

Breda shrugged and clasped her hands before her. "That isn't for me to decide. I'm certain that would fall to you."

Death quirked a brow. "Have it figured out, do you?"

"You have an aura about you. It's unmistakable. The only thing I don't know is who he is," Breda said about the man.

He chuckled and exchanged a look with Death. "I'm Cael."

"He was once my right hand and led the Reapers," Erith said as she reached for his hand. "Then we fell in love. Unfortunately, he paid the price when we battled an enemy. Cael nearly died but somehow took some of my magic and saved himself. He's no longer Fae. He's a god."

So that explained his eyes. Dozens of questions popped into Breda's mind. Her lips parted, but she got control of her curiosity and remained quiet.

"I am Death," the woman said as she returned her gaze to Breda. "Those closest to me know me as Erith."

Breda shifted uncomfortably. "I'm not sure you should've told me any of that."

"Oh?" Cael asked with a raised brow.

"The Six will want information. They'll find a way to get it out of me."

Erith smiled. "I'm sure they'll try."

Breda looked from Death to Cael. She wasn't sure she liked where this was going. "What do you mean?"

"This is our chance to find the Others. We're all going," Cael stated.

Breda spun and looked at Torin. "No. Things could go wrong. Then they would have all of you, including Death."

"They can't hold me," Erith stated.

This couldn't be happening. Breda turned to Death and Cael.

"You've not seen what they can do. I'm sure you're very powerful, and maybe the Six are overextending themselves to think they can defeat any of you. But do you want to underestimate them?"

"She has a point," Balladyn said.

Cael's brow furrowed. "We could allow one team to accompany Breda, and once they confirm things, another can follow them in."

"It'll allow us to get a look at the holdings and see how many soldiers there are," Torin offered.

Erith lifted her chin. "Or I go in with Breda alone and get this over with immediately."

The men began talking at once.

Death lifted her hand, silencing them instantly. Her eyes never left Breda. She closed the distance between them until she stood a few steps away. "What do you think?"

"Me?" Breda asked in shock. "I know nothing about battle or war tactics. All I know is survival."

"That's the most important. It's gotten you this far."

Breda glanced away, but she was compelled to look at Erith. "I'm nobody. I've survived on sheer will alone."

"You wouldn't call yourself a warrior?"

She snorted and shook her head. "Not even close."

"Yet you're willing to put yourself into a perilous situation that may take your life in the end."

Breda thought of Torin, of the life she finally had to live for. "I'm doing the right thing because it falls to me. I don't want to do this, but I will."

Erith leaned close and said with a smile, "My dear, that's a warrior." She returned to Cael's side.

As if on cue, the Reapers from the other day suddenly appeared. Only Aisling was missing. Breda looked at each one, stopping finally at Torin. This was really about to happen. There was still time for her to change her mind, and while every fiber of her being begged her to call it off, her heart wouldn't let her.

"Oh, and Breda," Erith said, getting her attention. "Keep your shields up."

Breda nodded, swallowing hard.

Torin walked to her. He didn't ask her if she wanted to back out, and she was thankful for that. "I won't be able to touch you because I'll be veiled," he explained. "All of us will. If I touch you, then you'll vanish and alert the soldiers we're there. But I won't leave your side."

"How will I know you're there?"

"I will be," he promised.

She heard Erith talking, saying something about taking them to Earth instead of using the doorway, but Breda was too focused on Torin to listen. She rose on her tiptoes and grabbed his face for a quick kiss. "I love you," she whispered.

He winked at her before she released him, and then he disappeared. Breda turned around to find only Cael and Erith visible.

"The Reapers will protect you," Death told her.

Breda nodded, and in her next breath, she found herself back in Dublin beneath a partly cloudy sky at sunset.

CHAPTER TWENTY

He hated every second of this, but Torin understood why Breda was using herself as an enticement. That didn't mean he had to like it. His gut clenched at the panic etched on Breda's face. He wanted to go to her, to take her hand and tell her that it would be all right. But he wasn't the type to give false promises.

"Torin?" she whispered.

He moved right behind her. "I'm here," he answered softly.

Relief seemed to erase her fear, which helped loosen the band around his chest. Erith had put them in the Temple Bar district. The neighborhood spanned the riverside and spread over cobbled lanes. It was always busy because it was home to the most extensive whisky collection in Ireland. Live Irish music wafted from the open doors of the Temple Bar itself.

Streetlights flickered, reflecting on the many small puddles on the cobblestones. Their group was tucked behind a building to get their bearings. He could look down the alley and see the tourists' and locals' movements as they went about their business.

If the soldiers were hunting, Breda would never have to leave this area. It would be impossible for him to stay near Breda if she went onto the street. They were veiled, not ghosts, so if anyone bumped into them, they would feel a solid body, even if they didn't see anything. Torin didn't want to bring that kind of attention to himself.

Torin looked between Eoghan, Cathal, Rordan, Bradach, Dubhan, and Balladyn. They stood at the ready, just as he did. Torin realized they should've prepped Breda better, but then again, no one knew what to expect.

Though there was one thing the soldiers had done repeatedly.

Torin sidled up behind Breda, bending so his face was near her ear. "When the soldiers arrive, they're going to send a blast of magic to make sure no one is veiled."

"But…you are," she whispered.

He looked at the rooftops above him and pointed to them as he looked at the others. Eoghan nodded and motioned for everyone to teleport. "We've got that taken care of. Once the soldiers know you're alone, they'll grab you. Act like you would if you were alone. And remember, I'm right here."

She nodded and crossed her arms over her chest as she nervously tapped her toe. Her eyes darted about. The worst part of a scenario like this was the waiting—for everyone involved. Torin didn't leave her side, even though he was taking a chance by remaining. He had given her his word, and he wouldn't go back on it.

Breda's quick intake of breath alerted him that something had happened. He followed her gaze and saw the Fae dressed in all black. Five more appeared a second later. Torin barely jumped to the roof before the soldiers sent out their gusts of magic. A second and third soon followed in various locations, causing him and his brethren to get creative in their locations so as not to be hit with it.

Torin teleported to the sidewalk, quickly stepping to the side so as not to have a group of drunken men run into him. He ran up behind the soldiers and noted that of the five, only three were searching for anyone veiled. The other two had a hold of Breda. She fought them, kicking one in the balls.

The Light backhanded her so hard that it knocked her out. Torin lunged toward them only to have someone draw him up short. He glared at Balladyn and Cathal, but they didn't release him. Then the soldiers—along with Breda—were gone.

Cathal and Balladyn finally released him as the other four Reapers joined them. All Fae left trails of magic, though they usually weren't seen. The Reapers had that advantage. They were able to follow the soldiers' magic, which was the only reason Torin hadn't completely flipped out. He fisted his hands, yearning to punch the Fae who had dared to lay his hands on Breda.

Eoghan caught his attention and nodded. Torin returned the gesture, letting everyone know that he had control of his rage. For the time being, at least.

The Reapers, as a team, focused on the swirls of magic the soldiers had left behind in their wake. They didn't drop their veils or speak in case someone was watching. While they weren't sure what awaited them, they knew what to expect. And what to do.

The instant Eoghan motioned for them to follow the soldiers, Torin teleported, anxious to get to Breda. He found himself in a large, darkened building with lights coming down from the center, shining upon a platform that he spotted through the rows of bodies. He looked around for his team but only found the Fae. The stadium seating encircled the platform in the middle, and he was on the top row.

The room was eerily quiet. The Fae stood at attention, their gazes locked on the platform below. Torin didn't like his position. He couldn't walk because it would cause him to bump into someone. The last thing he wanted was to alert anyone that he was veiled. He contemplated teleporting to the platform, but something told him that wouldn't be the wisest choice.

Still, he couldn't remain there. He had promised Breda that he would be beside her. He wasn't, and that worried him.

Torin looked up to find several steel beams visible. Jumping down might not be wise, but he might be able to go up. It was still risky. He searched for his brethren once more so he could tell them his plan. When he couldn't find them, he teleported and balanced atop a beam in the open ceiling.

From this vantage point, he could see everything and everyone. Torin whispered each of the Reapers' names, and one-by-one, they jumped to him.

"Fek," Bradach murmured.

A muscle moved in Balladyn's jaw. "It's just as Breda described."

"She knew they would bring her here," Eoghan whispered.

Torin glared at the empty dais. "Where are they? Where is Breda?"

No sooner were the words out of his mouth than the Six appeared. Three Dark, three Light, all wearing white robes as they stood in a circle and faced each other. Torin looked down on them, which meant he couldn't get a good view of their faces.

"One of us needs to go back down," Dubhan whispered.

Eoghan held up a hand to silence him.

The seconds stretched to minutes as the Six stared at each other. Finally, the middle Light spoke.

"We have two surprises today."

Torin exchanged a look with Balladyn, both wondering if the Reapers were one of the surprises.

"We are a family," she continued. "It makes us very… annoyed…when one of ours tries to leave. We've gone to great lengths to impart truths that have been kept from us, truths that change our very existence. When we pledge to this organization, it's for life. We are your family."

Torin told himself to stay calm, but alarm and trepidation had tripled within him since their arrival. That same nauseating feeling he'd had on Achill Island that something bad was about to happen returned, and he knew exactly who it was for—Breda.

"Our sister lost her way, but we've brought her back into the fold," the Light stated.

Double doors to the left opened, and the soldiers who'd taken Breda led her in. Torin's gut clenched at the sight of her. He steeled himself for the torture he knew was coming, but the Fae stopped Breda before she reached the platform.

"We will get to our sister shortly. First, my second surprise," the female said, a smile in her voice.

Rordan made an indistinct noise when a male stepped through the same doors as Breda, though he was without guards. Torin looked from the Light to Rordan.

"It's Ruarc," Rordan said in a low voice.

Torin's head snapped around to watch the Light walk toward the dais. Rordan had been searching for his friend since they'd met on Achill Island, but Ruarc had disappeared without a trace. Rordan had long suspected that something had happened to Ruarc. Now, they knew.

"Welcome our newest brother," the leader stated.

The crowd erupted in applause. Ruarc bowed his head to the Six before walking to climb the stadium stairs to a position two-thirds of the way to the top.

"He wouldn't," Rordan murmured.

Torin looked at Eoghan and motioned to the Six.

Eoghan shook his head.

Torin glared at him, pointing to the Six again. "*Now*," he mouthed.

Eoghan held his gaze and shook his head again.

"Why?" Torin demanded, his voice barely a whisper.

It was Balladyn who said, "We need them focused on Breda."

In other words, the Six needed to be torturing her. Torin swung his gaze to Breda. He wasn't beside her as he'd promised. Had she said his name? Had she reached out a hand for him? It tore him up that she might have done those things and more, looking for him to reassure her, and he hadn't.

Because he hadn't been there.

It was bad enough that she was even here. He wouldn't allow her to be brutalized on top of that. He didn't care if it went against Death's wishes or not. Breda had experienced enough in her life. She had willingly put herself out there so the Reapers could find the Others, and how were they going to repay that courage? By allowing her to feel pain.

"It was her idea," Balladyn whispered.

Torin jerked his head to Balladyn before looking at Eoghan, who nodded in answer. Of course, she would tell them that. Because she wanted the Reapers to end the Six once and for all. He ran a hand down his face in frustration. It took every ounce of control he had to keep himself in check. He wouldn't be able to watch her being hurt.

He realized that his brethren were watching him. Torin knew what he had to do, but that didn't mean he liked it.

Dubhan motioned below. Torin swung his head to find the soldiers moving away from Breda. He knew what was coming. He couldn't fill his lungs with air. His beautiful Breda was about to endure horrific pain—so the Reapers could put an end to them.

She lifted her chin, glaring at the Six. They never looked at her. Torin waited for them to do something, but they simply stood there. He frowned as he watched the soldiers who had brought her in call to their magic. Torin's stomach clenched with dread. He wished he could send strength to Breda. She was unbelievably strong but not nearly enough for what was coming.

The two soldiers let their magic merge. The iridescent colors coalesced and began swirling as the orb expanded at a rapid rate. It built to the point where the building started to vibrate. Torin glanced up at his fellow Reapers, who all wore expressions of worry and shock.

Suddenly, Breda levitated a few inches off the floor. Fear clouded her face as she fought to get her balance, but her body was being controlled. The Six each took two steps back as Breda floated to the middle of the platform between them.

Torin shook his head. He couldn't do this. He couldn't stand back and watch the woman he loved get hurt. His lips parted to tell Eoghan exactly that when the soldiers turned the full force of their magic on Breda. The scream that rent the air was so full of pain and anguish that Torin's knees buckled, the sound searing into his mind for eternity.

Strong hands gripped his shoulders, keeping him in place. He didn't look at his friends. He tried to shake off their hold so he could get to Breda, but he couldn't get free. It was the look that passed between the soldiers that made his stomach plummet to his feet, because he realized their plan too late.

"No," he whispered.

The soldiers wore smiles of triumph as they walked to Breda and touched her. Her screams halted instantly, the agony replaced with…rage.

Torin used his magic to shove his friends aside and jumped to the dais.

CHAPTER TWENTY-ONE

Focus on a point. You know what's coming. You can handle it.

Breda repeated the words to herself, beginning the moment the soldiers took her. She didn't look for Torin, didn't say his name, didn't do anything that would alert anyone that someone might be there.

And it had been the most challenging thing she had ever done.

Knowing that he was there gave her the courage to keep her chin up and her back straight. Even when they brought her into the main chamber. The fact that the Six made her anxiety grow with the wait as they introduced a new member to the organization was another reason they were wankers.

Her heart had been beating fast for so long, she feared the organ might give out completely. That would definitely put a crimp in the arseholes' plans. The thought brought a slight grin to her lips, but it faded when she felt everyone's attention on her. Her gaze moved around the room to all the Fae staring. That's when she saw her mother's face, the satisfied smile wide.

Torin had been right. Her mother had told the Six what she was. Breda parted her lips to shout a warning to Torin and the others when she found herself lifted off the floor. Worse was the knowledge that she had lost control of her body.

Breda began to shake violently from the panic coursing through her. She tried not to cry, but she couldn't stop the tears from falling. All the reasons why she had put herself in this predicament seemed ridiculous now. She wanted to be back on the Fae Realm, safe in Torin's arms. But she was well past that now.

Light blinded her as they moved her to the middle of the dais. No longer could she see the audience members' faces. What little nerve she had to stare at the Six vanished in her effort to remain as composed as she could—though it was a losing battle.

She had no idea what to expect because every torture had been different. But the one thing she knew for certain was that it would be ghastly.

Breda drew in a deep breath and was in the process of releasing it when the pain consumed her. Try as she might, she couldn't hold back her scream. Her entire body felt as if it were on fire—burning from the inside out. She tried to move, to thrash, but she couldn't budge. Another wave of it slammed into her. She squeezed her eyes shut, wondering where Torin was. She might have told Eoghan and Balladyn to wait until the torture began, but she'd thought they would rescue her right after.

Unless they couldn't.

Unless they hadn't followed her.

Tears streamed down Breda's face.

As quickly as the pain engulfed her, it ended. Replaced by unimaginable fury. She needed to hurt. Kill. Her feet met the floor, and she once more had control of her body. The instant Torin dropped his veil, she locked gazes with him. Deep in her heart, she knew that she didn't want to hurt him, but she couldn't stop herself.

The sound of Breda's screams was like daggers to Torin's heart. He'd never wanted to fight more than he did at that moment. And he was going after the ones responsible for harming his woman.

He dropped his veil as he landed behind two of the Six. Torin kicked the back of the Light female's knee, causing her to pitch forward. He grabbed her hair and jerked back before slamming a ball of magic into her face.

Shrieks of shock and fear erupted around him as Fae tried to flee. His surprise arrival was enough to give him time to attack, but the soldiers turned their magic on him. Torin lifted the Light, using her as a shield. Her cries were cut short as she crumbled to ash. Before he could turn to the next Other, magic slammed into his chest. He looked up, shocked to see Breda hurling magic at him.

Suddenly, his fellow Reapers were beside him.

Torin grimaced as orb after orb pummeled him. He instantly began healing from Breda's attack, but her magic didn't hurt as much as the attack itself. He knew she wasn't doing this, though— the soldiers and the Six were. Torin rushed to Breda to stop her when he heard laughter.

He looked over to see the remaining Six watching him. The tall Light was the one laughing. By their looks, they had discovered exactly what Breda was and had used her against the Reapers.

Another ball of magic hit Torin in the neck as he paused to consider going after the Six. Before he could, they vanished, and soldiers rushed in from everywhere. The frightened onlookers quickly teleported away.

Torin swung his head to Breda to see her gathering more magic. He rushed her, tackling her to the floor and pinning her arms before she could throw the orb. "Breda," he called.

"Get off me!" she screamed while trying to knock him aside.

The Reapers formed a circle around him and Breda, facing the soldiers moving in to surround them.

"This is going to be fun," Balladyn said.

Bradach grunted. "I've been waiting for this for some time."

Torin glanced up. The Reapers were outnumbered, ten to one. They might be Reapers, but they could be killed. There was no coming back for them if they died a second time. This entire ordeal had been a trap. The Six had somehow known that the Reapers had helped Breda. Breda's family had likely alerted the

Others to her power, and the Six had decided to use it against the Reapers.

He looked down at the woman who had stolen his heart. The hatred on her face made his heart catch, but he knew it wasn't her emotions. It was the soldiers'.

"Breda, listen to me," Torin said as she fought. "Those aren't your emotions. Put your shields back up."

She kneed him in the back and bucked her hips, but he didn't budge.

"Fight!" he bellowed.

His voice startled her enough that she stilled and blinked up at him. Confusion filled her visage. "Torin?"

He breathed a sigh of relief. "Is it you?"

Fresh tears filled her red eyes. "I hurt you."

"Breda," he said, shaking her arms. "Is it you? Are you in control?"

She nodded.

"Stay down," he warned. "Things are going to get rough."

Torin jumped to his feet as a soldier let out a bellow and rushed the dais. He dodged three orbs aimed at him, but the fourth and fifth found their marks on his right thigh and left arm. The soldiers were good, but they didn't compare to the training the Reapers had.

Torin blocked out the pain as he took out the two soldiers nearest him. His right knee buckled, sending him to the floor as another volley of magic hit him. He let out a bellow and lunged toward a soldier near him, about to throw an orb at Dubhan. Torin slammed a bubble of magic into the soldier's back, severing his spine and turning him to ash.

After Torin managed to get to his feet, balancing on his one good leg, he killed two more soldiers.

～

Shame and mortification filled Breda. It had all been a trap for the Reapers. Her vision blurred with tears as her head turned to Torin.

She remembered feeling such hatred for him that she had wanted him dead.

And she had attacked him.

She saw the wounds from her assault. Her shields had failed, but then again, she hadn't thought about them when she was in pain. The Six had, however. They had used her to get the upper hand with the Reapers.

But no longer. Breda gritted her teeth as she rolled onto her side and pushed herself up. She wasn't a Reaper, didn't have their skills or the additional magic from Death, but she was partly responsible for this catastrophe, and she would do her part.

Her body throbbed from the torture, however brief it had been, but she ignored it and pushed into a sitting position as she gathered her magic between her hands. An orb quickly formed. Her head swiveled as she took stock of the Reapers. All of them had suffered wounds. Out of the corner of her eye, she spotted a ball of magic coming for Eoghan. She lifted her orb to throw it at the soldier as Eoghan ducked. Breda rolled away as the ball continued on its course, directly for her.

But she wasn't fast enough. The magic landed on her hand and wrist. Fae magic was like acid. It sank through skin, muscle, and into bone, burning everything it touched. Her arm shook from the agony. Her head jerked to the wound. When she saw bone, she pulled her arm against her to protect the injury as best she could. A Fae could heal from such a wound given time. But she had human blood, so she didn't know if she could heal completely.

Her gaze went to Torin when she saw him fall to one knee. His clothes were riddled with burn marks from the shots of magic that had found their way to him. She didn't know how he was mostly still standing, much less continuing to battle. As she watched, he took out a soldier about to attack Dubhan. When he struggled to get to his feet, she willed him the ability to do it. Then he killed two more soldiers. She smiled, watching him with awe.

As he was about to throw an orb, he was struck from behind. She called his name as he fell forward, catching himself with his hands. Soldiers rushed him. Breda threw a couple of balls of magic

at the soldiers as she willed Torin to get up again. It looked like he
was going to do it, but then his arms gave out. The soldiers crowded
around him so she could no longer see him.

"Torin!" she bellowed.

All of this had been her idea, but only because she was
expendable. Torin wasn't. She couldn't lose him now. Breda forgot
all about her injury and used both hands to send a blast of magic
toward the soldier. It found its mark, but the soldier didn't even turn
to her.

A second later, she heard a loud bellow, and the soldiers went
flying in all directions, leaving Torin standing with his hand around
the throat of one soldier while throwing orbs with the other.

"Erith," Breda whispered, hoping the goddess heard her.

Torin was nearly at his limit. He glanced around to see that his
fellow Reapers had killed many soldiers, but all of the Reapers were
severely injured, as well. As Torin turned back around, his gaze
landed on Breda to find her looking at him. When she smiled, he
felt such a rush of emotion that it dulled the pain of his wounds.

"Behind you!" she shouted.

He spun around to throw two orbs from each hand before
rolling to the side and coming up on his good knee to toss two more.
A ball came at Torin's head that barely missed. As he turned in the
direction where it had come from, Erith, Cael, and the other group
of Reapers appeared. In minutes, no soldiers remained.

Torin used the edge of the dais to stand. He leaned his weight
on his uninjured leg and limped as quickly as he could to Breda.

"Hey," she said with a grin.

He returned her smile. "Hey."

"I'm sorry," she cried.

He gently caught her tears with his thumb. "It wasn't your fault.
None of it."

"One of you could've been killed."

That's when Torin saw the damage to her hand. She was also

wounded on her hip and two places on her lower leg. Torin couldn't wait to leave this place. "What did they do to you?" He felt the need to gather her in his arms, but the last thing he wanted was to hurt her more.

Breda was pale, her lips tight from pain. "It doesn't matter. They did enough that I forgot about my shields."

"Which was what they wanted," Erith stated.

"We could've used you sooner," Cathal said as he walked up, breathing hard.

Cael grunted. "We would've been here sooner had one of you called. Thankfully, Breda did."

Torin exchanged looks with his team. "We were a little preoccupied."

"It doesn't matter. The soldiers are dead," Daire replied.

Erith looked at Eoghan. "And the Six?"

"Torin killed one, but the other five got away," Eoghan answered.

"It was a setup," Balladyn said.

Breda nodded slowly. "I saw my mother with the other Fae."

"Fek," Torin mumbled. He'd had a feeling that Breda's family would make a move. He hated that he'd been right.

Rordan sat down heavily on the edge of the dais. "To make matters worse, we scared the hell out of the Fae that were here."

"That's going to fan the fire the Others already started," Fintan said, his red-rimmed white eyes taking in the place.

Rordan ran a hand through his hair. "Ruarc was here."

"He's one of them," Bradach added.

Rordan shook his head. "He wouldn't have willingly joined."

"You can't know that," Dubhan replied.

Rordan shot him a hard look. "I can. I trusted Ruarc when I was on Achill Island. He didn't like the direction things were headed at the meetings, but he was forced to attend. Does that sound like someone who wanted to join?"

A sound suddenly had everyone on their feet, their eyes locked on a solitary figure. But it wasn't a soldier who came out of the darkness. It was a Fae.

"Ruarc," Rordan said and started toward him.

The Light barely looked at Rordan. Instead, Ruarc's gaze landed on Erith before moving to Cael.

To Torin's surprise, Erith motioned for the Reapers to move aside so he could pass. Ruarc slowly walked away, never looking at any of them again. Once Ruarc was through the doors, Cael turned to his group of Reapers.

"We need to check the facility and see what's here," he told them.

When Cael and his team were gone, Torin bent to help Breda to her feet. That's when he found his brethren facing her.

"What you did goes beyond anything I've seen," Eoghan said. "We can never thank you enough."

Breda flushed under the praise, making Torin smile. "I was used. And the Six got away."

"Not all of them," Erith said as she caught Torin's eye.

Balladyn grinned. "We let them know we can find them."

"They'll strike against us quickly," Bradach pointed out.

Dubhan chuckled. "Bring it on."

Torin's wounds were mending, but Breda's were taking longer. "I need to get Breda away."

"Take her," Erith said. "All of you go and heal. We need to prepare for what comes next."

Balladyn grunted. "It's going to be a doozy, whatever it is."

Torin linked his fingers with Breda's good hand. He didn't want to think about the Others, not now. Breda was alive. He was alive. Right now, that was enough.

CHAPTER TWENTY-TWO

Xaneth clenched his hands in anger as he stared at Death and the Reapers. They had beaten him to the evil. He should be glad they'd helped rid the realm of such malevolence, but he wasn't. It was his duty.

They had intervened.

He followed the gazes of those within the room to the Light Fae who came out of the shadows. Xaneth sniffed the air but didn't smell evil on the male. Despite Cathal calling out to the Light, the male kept walking. Xaneth stepped out of view so when Ruarc walked out, he didn't see him.

There was nothing for Xaneth here any longer. He had sensed a tremendous amount of evil that'd led him to this place. He'd been excited to stamp out the wickedness. The ash covering the floor told him that numerous evil Fae had been slain. But it wasn't the ones who had originally led him here. They were still out there.

And he would find them.

He'd wanted to look around the compound, but the instant he heard Cael give the order for the Reapers to check the place, Xaneth had no choice but to leave. He peered around the corner to look at the Reapers once more. His gaze searched for long, black and silver braids. Disappointment pierced him when he didn't see her. Though, he knew it was better this way.

Xaneth teleported out of the building and back to the warehouse. He paced, trying to dispel the pent-up energy, but it didn't help. A dull ache began at the back of his head near the base of his neck. He closed his eyes and drew in a deep breath, hoping to catch a whiff of evil. The instant he caught the scent, he followed the odor. The stench led him to a residential area of the city. His feet were silent on the cobblestones as music from nearby pubs and loud conversations drowned out everything else.

Thick, low-lying clouds moved rapidly across the sky, blocking out the moon for several seconds at a time. Xaneth ignored the people on the street—both human and Fae alike—as he hunted his quarry. He was locked onto the vile stench of wickedness, and nothing could distract him.

The closer he got, the worse the stink became. It was so revolting that it turned his stomach. He couldn't understand why no one else smelled it. Or was it that it didn't bother them as it did him? Those thoughts skidded to a halt when he heard the shrill scream of an animal in pain.

Xaneth started running. He skidded to a halt in front of a tall building. He teleported to the roof and scanned the area until he found them. Two teenage Darks tormenting a young Light female and her puppy. The teenagers were pummeling the small dog with magic to hear it yelp in pain. The Light did her best to shield the dog and herself, but both had been hit.

With his teeth bared, Xaneth jumped between the teenagers and the girl. The boys jerked back in surprise at the sight of him. "Leave," he ordered them.

One Dark stumbled as if considering it. The other lifted his chin. "You can't tell me to leave."

"I just did," Xaneth replied in a cool tone. The sound of the little girl crying behind him as the dog whimpered caused anger to burn hotly inside him. "What kind of Dark are you to torment a child and an animal? Were you never taught manners?"

The frightened Dark left without a word to his friend.

The other swallowed, puffing out his chest in an effort to appear tough. "Get off my property."

Xaneth narrowed his gaze on the teenager. "Yours?"

"My parents', yes."

Xaneth shifted to the side and dragged his gaze from the teenager to the girl. He looked between the two, seeing similar attributes. "Is that your sister?"

"Half-sister," the teenager retorted with a sneer.

Xaneth slid his gaze to the little girl to see her tear-streaked face. She watched Xaneth closely while holding her puppy. The child would likely eventually turn Dark like the rest of her family, but for now, she was an innocent and being cruelly tormented.

"Leave before my da returns," the teenager ordered.

Xaneth's head snapped back to him. He advanced on the Dark, satisfaction filling him when the teenager hurriedly stepped back, only to bump into a fence. Xaneth leaned close and sniffed, the disgusting smell of evil permeating from the Dark. "What did you intend tonight? To kill a puppy?"

"It's just a fekking animal."

"It's an innocent dog who can't defend itself."

The Dark shrugged indifferently. "So? I'm sure they'll get her another one."

"And your half-sister? How badly would you have harmed her?"

He sneered in contempt. "She'll survive."

Xaneth snorted. "Is it your jealousy over the fact that your father gives attention to someone else that makes you hate her so?"

"It's none of your bloody business."

Everything within Xaneth told him to end the Dark's life. His stench had led Xaneth to him, but he was just a kid. Xaneth held his gaze and leaned close so their noses were nearly touching. "She's your family. Protect her. Don't hurt her. Do you understand?"

The Dark nodded quickly, fear rolling off him in waves.

Xaneth released him and turned to the little girl. The puppy was barely breathing now, its white and tan fur charred from the blasts of magic. He walked to her, squatting before her to gently place his hand on the dog. Xaneth wanted nothing more than to heal the animal, or at least take away its pain. He'd barely brushed his fingers across the fur when pain seared his back.

Without hesitation, he turned and threw an orb at the teenager, killing him instantly. Xaneth didn't watch him disintegrate. Instead, he focused his attention on the child, shielding her from the sight of her half-brother turning to ash.

"You're already healing," he told her in a soft voice.

She swallowed and sniffed loudly. "Fluffy isn't."

Xaneth rested his hand on the dog's head, intending to end its suffering. He closed his eyes, preparing himself to take the animal's life. Before he could, the girl sucked in a startled breath, almost at the same time Xaneth felt the puppy's head move. His eyes snapped open to see the dog's tail wagging as he tried to lick the girl's face. To Xaneth's shock, the puppy's wounds were healed.

The child giggled as the dog licked her. She set Fluffy on the ground then threw herself against Xaneth, hugging him tightly with her pudgy arms. "Thank you," she whispered.

He was so shocked by her embrace that he didn't know what to do. He didn't like being touched, but he couldn't force her away. Finally, hesitantly, he placed a hand on her back for the barest of seconds. Then she bolted out of his hold as she and Fluffy raced back inside the house. He straightened upon hearing the front door open. When he heard the girl call out for her parents, Xaneth teleported to the roof and hid behind the chimney as the three came outside.

"He was right here," the child said.

The woman asked, "Who?"

"He saved me and Fluffy," the girl answered.

A deep voice asked, "Saved you from who?"

"Teddy," she said in a small voice. "He was hurting me and Fluffy again. See."

Xaneth peeked around to see the girl holding out her arms, showing her parents the healing wounds.

"He warned Teddy to stop hurting us, but then Teddy hurt him. So, he made Teddy stop forever."

The woman gathered the child in her arms, holding her tightly as she and the father looked around in fear.

"Gail," the man said in a strangled voice. "There's ash here."

"Teddy," the girl said.

The two adults exchanged a look before the woman rushed inside with the girl. The man lingered, his gaze moving around the area before lifting to the rooftop. Xaneth flattened himself against the chimney. He had stamped out evil, but it wasn't the kind he usually sought.

His headache intensified. He had to get out of sight. Xaneth barely teleported back to the warehouse before he collapsed to the floor.

She had never been so furious. Breda had been working with the Reapers. And the foul monsters had found them. They shouldn't have been able to get into the complex. She would have to rectify that.

"What do we do now?"

"I knew it was only a matter of time."

"We need to hide."

"We can't hide now."

"Enough!" she bellowed to the other four. She looked at them. "It was only a matter of time before we encountered the Reapers. We knew it was a chance, which is why we set the trap."

Dark 2 flattened her lips. "A trap that didn't work."

"We were supposed to attack the Reapers on our schedule," Dark 1 said.

She glared at him before moving her gaze to the two Dark females and the other Light. "They used Breda to find us. Thanks to Breda's mother, we were able to turn the tide to our advantage."

"I wouldn't call losing one of us an advantage," Light 2 stated.

She took a calming breath. "We have the perfect replacement."

"You can't be serious," Dark 3 replied in shock.

She grinned. "Ruarc is perfect."

"You're playing a dangerous game," Light 2 said.

She twisted her lips as she shrugged. "Did you see the fear on everyone's faces when the Reapers arrived? Everything we've told them about that group was proven today. Whether the Reapers know it or not, they played right into our hands. Now, we take advantage of that."

The others looked at each other before reluctantly nodding in agreement. She smiled in anticipation. This had gone better than she could've hoped. Her next idea would end the Reapers once and for all.

CHAPTER TWENTY-THREE

Breda opened her eyes and discovered that she was in the tent. She turned her head, searching for Torin, but he wasn't there. She then took stock of her body. Thankfully, there were only a few lingering twinges from her injuries.

She sat up and swung her legs over the side of the bed. As she walked to the entrance, she strained her ears to hear talking but was met with only silence. Worry filled her when she shoved aside the curtain and emerged into the common area. It was empty, as were the two other rooms.

Breda faced the main entrance, her heart thumping wildly in fear. Had Torin left? Without a farewell? He'd told her that he loved her. She had told him the same. Didn't that mean something? She rushed out of the tent, her head on a swivel as she searched. She jogged to the river, continuing to look for him.

"Torin?"

If he were on the Fae Realm, he would hear her and come. Hopefully.

Maybe.

She turned in a circle, looking for someone, anyone. It didn't take her long to come to the conclusion that she was alone. At least, they left her on the Fae Realm instead of Earth. She had a chance of hiding here. It was just that…

"I thought we'd get to say goodbye."

She supposed she had held up her end of the bargain. In exchange, Death had let her go. Though with everything Breda knew, she was surprised.

"Then again, who am I going to tell here?" she asked as she threw up her hands and let them fall to her thighs in defeat.

"Do you always talk to yourself?"

She spun around at the sound of a voice to find Erith. Breda didn't know whether to be happy that she might find out what was going on, or afraid that Death may kill her.

"I'm judge and jury. My Reapers are the executioners."

Breda pulled back. "What?"

"Your dread was written all over your face. I merely pointed out a fact. Come," Erith said as she turned on her heel and entered the tent.

Breda hesitated for only a heartbeat before following. After ducking inside, she straightened, hoping to find Torin. Again, she was disappointed. Realizing that might show on her face, Breda glanced at Erith. The goddess quirked a brow and motioned to the sofa as she sat.

Breda's hands were clammy as she walked on wooden legs to the opposite side of the sofa and lowered herself onto the edge of the cushion. She swallowed nervously as she and Erith stared at each other.

"You could've died," Death finally said.

"I could have."

"Are you disappointed that you didn't?"

Breda blinked, taken aback. "Ah. No. I'm quite happy to have made it out alive. I just don't want any of you thinking I was part of the trap."

"Rest easy about that."

Whew. She hadn't realized how scared she was about that until then. "So…what happens now?"

"What would you like to happen?"

She started to answer, then shook her head as she shrugged. "I don't know."

"Yes, you do."

Breda looked away as she thought of Torin. What she wanted was to be with him. To wake up in his arms each day—see his smile, feel his touch, hear his voice. She wanted to know every detail of his life and share everything about hers. But she wasn't a Reaper. How could she have all of that and be with Torin when she wasn't one of them?

Finally, she looked at Erith and said, "I don't think I can have what I want."

"You'll never know unless you go after it. Tell me what it is."

Why couldn't Breda say it? But she knew why. She had been set up for disappointment so many times that she couldn't handle another one—not when it came to Torin.

"Breda," Death urged. "Say it."

"I don't think I can."

Erith shot her a dry look. "This coming from a woman who stood against the Others and took the torture of the soldiers without hesitation? You have more courage than you give yourself credit for."

"Well, when you put it like that, I kinda have to say it."

"Exactly," Death stated with a knowing look.

Breda took a deep breath and slowly released it as she rubbed her sweaty palms on her jean-clad thighs. "I want to be with Torin. I love him. We fell in love. I mean, he loves me. At least, that's what he said. I know it's fast and probably unrealistic but—"

"Stop talking, Breda."

Breda halted, grasping that she had been rambling. But once the words started, she hadn't been able to stop them.

"I've talked at length with Torin. I wanted a chance to speak with you, as well."

Breda twisted her hands in her lap as her nervousness grew. "What did he say?"

"Essentially what you did."

A laugh of happiness escaped. Breda slapped a hand over her

mouth. Never in her life had she giggled before, but there was no other word for the sound that had come from her. She composed herself and straightened her back as she clasped her hands in her lap.

"As I was saying," Erith continued, "your sacrifice has been noted. Not just with me but with all the Reapers. You've told Torin you don't feel as if you fit in the human or Fae world. I think you'll find you have a place in ours."

For a moment, Breda didn't move. She wasn't sure she had heard correctly. "Are you...are you saying I can be with Torin? That's allowed?"

Erith laughed as she got to her feet. "Oh, yes. For those who prove their worthiness to my Reapers, it certainly is. And you, my dear, have more than proven yourself."

Breda jumped to her feet when Erith walked from the tent. She hurried after her. "Wait. What happens now?"

Erith paused and turned to her with a grin. "I think you'll find what you're looking for at the lake."

Breda felt her smile forming.

"I'll see you soon," Erith said and vanished.

Breda didn't waste any time running toward the lake. She wished she could teleport and get there faster. When she reached the cliff, she was out of breath. She glanced up and groaned. While she might have enjoyed climbing it the first time, all she wanted was to be with Torin now.

She closed her eyes and willed herself to be at the top. It was ridiculous, she knew, but she had to give herself a moment to catch her breath anyway. Except when she opened her eyes, she *was* at the top of the cliff.

Breda couldn't believe it. And the person she wanted to share it with was at the lake. She started running down the mountain to the valley, her eyes locked on the figure in the water. By the time she reached the shore, she had used magic to remove her clothes. Torin dipped beneath the water without seeing her.

She splashed into the lake, dove under, and started swimming. When she spotted him, she smiled and swam faster. He turned then and saw her. In the next instant, he was before her, his lips on hers. He grabbed her against him and pushed them up so they broke the surface.

"You're here," he said between kisses.

She laughed and lifted her face to the sun before looking at him. "I feared I'd never see you again."

"Leaving you was the hardest thing I've ever done, but Erith wanted to speak with you alone."

"She's very intense."

Torin nodded, grinning. "That she is."

Breda wiped the water from her face then wrapped her arms around his neck. "Are we going to live here?"

"We'll live on Death's realm with the others. I asked for a few days alone here with you."

"I didn't peg you for a romantic," she said. "But I heartily approve."

He gave her a lingering kiss. "I like to keep you on your toes."

She gazed into his silver eyes. "I can't believe you love me."

"I'm going to spend the rest of my life showing you just how much," he promised.

Tears filled her eyes and fell onto her cheeks. "I've never felt so safe, protected, or cared for as I do when I'm with you."

"It was seeing how you embraced each day despite your past that allowed me to let go of mine. There's no one like you in all the universe."

"You, my handsome Reaper, are my other half. I love you so much."

His hands splayed across her back as he lowered his head to hers.

EPILOGUE

Four days later…

"Wow," Breda said as Torin led her through the doorway to Death's realm—her new home.

The Fae Realm had been beautiful, but this place was so stunning that she couldn't find words. She could've spent hours walking among the different flowers near the doorway listening to the birds and other creatures, but Torin had dragged her away.

"You can look later," he said with a smile.

She gave the garden a lingering stare before facing forward and catching sight of the white tower.

"That is where Erith and Cael reside," Torin told her.

As they drew closer, she saw a large group of people waiting for her. She nodded to Torin's group of Reapers and was surprised to find that Eoghan, Bradach, Dubhan, Cathal, and Rordan all had women beside them. Torin introduced her to Thea, Maeve, Kyra, Sorcha, and Fianna.

Between the two groups stood Erith and Cael, both of which smiled in greeting. She didn't get a chance to speak to them as Torin turned her to the second group.

"This is Baylon and his mate, Jordan. There's Kyran and his wife, River, along with their son. Next is Talin and Neve, Fintan and Catriona, then Daire and Ettie."

Breda smiled and nodded to all of them. It was difficult not to notice that Balladyn stood slightly apart from the others and alone. There was still no sign of Aisling, either. Breda didn't get to linger on such thoughts as they sat beneath the shade of a large tree at a long table to accommodate them all.

The easy banter and laughter shared around the table quickly put her at ease. Breda even caught Balladyn laughing a time or two. Sometime during the meal, she realized that Death hadn't just allowed her to spend her life with Torin. Erith had opened their home and let her into their family.

Torin twined his fingers with hers beneath the table. "What are you thinking about?"

"That I've longed for a family my entire life."

"You have one now."

"I do," she said with a smile.

And just like that, she released her anger and grudges against her mother and grandmother. There wasn't room in her heart for such hatred and anger when so much love surrounded her.

Aisling wanted to howl in frustration. She had found Xaneth. He shouldn't have seen her since she was veiled, but he had. There was no doubt about it. Before she could say anything, he had vanished.

Into the pub's back rooms that no one but a Reaper should be able to teleport into and out of. What the bloody hell was going on? More pressing was that she had no idea where Xaneth was now. But she wouldn't give up.

"I'll find you yet," she vowed as she left the Sly Stag.

Thank you for reading DARK ALPHA'S NEED! I hope you loved

Torin and Breda's story as much as I loved writing it. Next up in the Dark World is the Reaper Christmas book, DARK ALPHA'S SILENT NIGHT.

Buy DARK ALPHA'S SILENT NIGHT now at
https://dgrant.co/3h8v27k

~

To find out when new books release
SIGN UP FOR MY NEWSLETTER today at
http://www.tinyurl.com/DonnaGrantNews.

Join my Facebook group, Donna Grant Groupies, for exclusive giveaways and sneak peeks of future books. If you loved the Dragon King series, you'll be thrilled to know Cullen gets his HEA in the next book, DRAGON UNBOUND…

He's never been tempted…until her.

Buy DRAGON UNBOUND now at
https://dgrant.co/3dlCkmr

Keep reading for a excerpt from DARK ALPHA'S SILENT NIGHT and a second bonus excerpt from DRAGON UNBOUND…

EXCERPT OF DARK ALPHA'S SILENT NIGHT

REAPERS, BOOK 13

New York Times **bestselling author Donna Grant gives us an intimate peek into the Reapers' new life with an all-new, heartwarming holiday tale...**

There is no escaping the Reapers. We are elite assassins, part of a brotherhood that only answers to Death. But when Death says it's our time to live, we are more than happy to obey.

We have suffered betrayal, heartbreak, chaos, and even death. Despite another foe lurking around the corner, most of us have found happiness and love. While some still search, there *is* contentment—a sense of peace and purpose. And with the holidays upon us, it is time to celebrate the family we have made. The one we chose. The season is for revelry, and we intend to take advantage. Whatever may come next will still be there after the last present is

~

River glanced over her shoulder and winked at Kyran as she left their house. She still couldn't believe she had fallen in love with a Reaper. Being a Halfling—half-human, half-Fae—had made for a difficult life growing up. She didn't belong in the Fae world because her blood was tainted. The human world only saw the beauty of a Fae and tried to exploit it. That's why she had attempted to hide who she was. Not to mention, she had gotten the family's gift. The ability to read ancient Fae languages. Something that only happened once a generation.

She learned not just of her family's legacy but also how to defend herself. She'd had no choice but to become a warrior. River both hated and liked that she had Fae blood. Since Kyran, she had come to terms with who she was and how she could use it to help Death and the Reapers.

Her steps were light as she walked. Death's realm was picturesque in every sense of the word. Every single place on the realm was jaw-droppingly gorgeous. She and Kyran had settled on a section of rolling hills near a loch. The minute he saw it, he just stopped and stared. He hadn't had to say a word. It was clear he was taken by it. She had known immediately that this was where he wanted to have a home.

After he became a Reaper, he and the others had moved about constantly, setting up temporary quarters on Earth. He hadn't had a real home in many centuries. Seeing how enamored he was with the location made it the perfect place for their home. The other Reapers found similar places.

Some were farther from the white tower that Erith and Cael used as their home, but she and Kyran were one of the closest to it. She didn't have the ability to teleport as the Reapers did, so she had to walk. River enjoyed having the time to herself—and the exercise. She shivered slightly in the cool, damp air, deciding that before she did anything, she should speak to Erith. This was Death's realm, after all.

Forty minutes later, River reached the white tower. She lifted her hand to knock, but the door opened before she got the chance. She found herself staring into Cael's purple eyes. The once-Light Fae had previously been the leader of Kyran's group of Reapers. After an altercation with one of his enemies where he nearly died—only to be saved by Erith's magic—he'd been transformed into a god.

"River," Cael greeted her with a smile. "What brings you to our door?"

"I was hoping I could talk with you and Erith."

He stepped aside so she could enter. "Of course."

River glanced up at the curving staircase that ran along one of the tower's walls, all the way to the very top. She spotted Erith midway up, making her way down the steps. Her long, blue-black hair was in a loose plait over one shoulder. The petite goddess effortlessly glided down the steps in an all-black outfit that was a cross between *Xena: Warrior Princess* and Hela from *Thor*. Somehow, Erith pulled it off in only a manner that Death could.

"What can we do for you?" Erith asked when she reached the bottom.

River took a deep breath and said, "I'm missing some of the things we did on Earth. I was hoping to throw a holiday dinner like what Con and Rhi did at Dreagan. Just for us here," she hastily added.

Erith's lavender gaze briefly moved to Cael before she said, "I think that would be delightful. With everything we've been dealing with, I'm sorry to say I haven't thought about what those of you who came here left behind."

"You have our gratitude for opening your home to us. We might miss a few things from Earth, but that can be remedied."

Cael walked to stand beside Erith. "I think a dinner party is just what we need."

"Yes," Erith said with a smile that didn't quite reach her eyes.

River understood. Their enemies had gotten powerful. Then there was the fact they chasing Xaneth—a royal Fae who had helped them. On top of that, Aisling had gone in search of him. Erith wasn't just looking for one person now but two. All of that weighed heavily on her slim shoulders.

That's when River realized that it wasn't just her that needed a night to remember what they had. Erith did, too.

All of them did.

~

Buy DARK ALPHA'S SILENT NIGHT now at
https://dgrant.co/3h8v27k

EXCERPT OF DRAGON UNBOUND
DRAGON KINGS, BOOK 3

In a new story brimming with sizzling heat and untold mysteries, *New York Times* bestselling author Donna Grant brings together a devilishly handsome Dragon King and a woman who dares to challenge him.

He's never been tempted...until her.

Sexy. Mysterious. Dangerous. He's an immortal Dragon King bound by ancient rules and eternal magic. Cullen has one objective: find and destroy the evil that threatens the new home of the dragons. Just when he's closing in, he's ambushed and finds a stunning warrior woman fighting alongside him. No amount of magic could prepare him for the beguiling lass who spurns his advances and defies him.

From the moment Tamlyn takes a stand against her kind, she's had to fight one perilous battle after another. Staying alive is an endless struggle, and the lines between good and evil are blurred with every encounter. She's always stood alone—until she comes to the aid of an irresistibly handsome stranger. Cullen will force her to face truths she's been running from…even as enemies plot to destroy them both.

This was Cullen's favorite time of day. He loved seeing the sunlight chase away the darkness and bathe the world in its radiance. But, most of all, he loved being able to fly freely. It wasn't something any of the Dragon Kings had been able to do in eons, not since they sent the dragons away and hid from the mortals.

His heart was both joyful and wrenched at the same time. The fact that these dragons were the descendants of those on Earth brought a smile to his face. Just as it did knowing they were safe and free to live as they were supposed to.

On the other hand, his gut churned with bitterness and regret that the Kings had once had a world like Zora, but things had gone badly, leaving them only one choice. Sadness weighed heavily upon him at what he and the other Kings had lost. Their world might not have been perfect, but it was as close as it could be in his eyes. Earth was a place where he had to search to find beauty. Something that had once been everywhere before the humans cut down forests, drained lakes, moved rivers, and blasted mountains, all to cover it with concrete and build shopping malls or houses. How much longer could it continue before they depleted Earth of all her resources? What would the tedious, wrathful mortals do then?

Cullen's thoughts skidded to a halt when he caught sight of a dark-haired woman bursting from the forest on the human side of the barrier with a small boy with black hair. They were running, the woman looking over her shoulder often. Cullen suspected the duo was coming for dragon territory, and since humans weren't supposed to cross over, it meant that he had to stop them.

Just as he dipped his wing to turn around and confront the pair, a group of armored and uniformed men poured from the forest. Many had some form of injury—blood covering nearly all of them. Cullen wasn't sure whose blood it was, but it didn't matter. The men were after the woman and child. No human was supposed to come onto dragon land, but he wasn't going to stand by and watch the men attack defenseless people.

Cullen tucked his wings and dove from the sky. As he neared, he opened his mouth and released his power of fog. It poured from him, falling to the ground and slowly spreading. He glanced at the woman and lad to see them near the edge of the barrier. His attention returned to the men. He curled into a ball as he shifted, calling his clothes and weapons to him as he landed on his feet.

Slowly, he lifted his head and grinned. He could see clearly through the fog, but the soldiers couldn't. They were disoriented and trying to discern where it had come from. Cullen remained still and, with a simple thought, dispersed the fog enough for the men to see him.

"Who the bloody hell are you?" one of the soldiers demanded.

Cullen let his gaze move over the group as he held his axe in his left hand and his sword in his right. "You have one chance to turn around and leave."

"Get out of our way," another ordered.

Cullen shrugged. "So be it."

～

Buy DRAGON UNBOUND now at
https://dgrant.co/3dlCkmr

ABOUT THE AUTHOR

New York Times and *USA Today* bestselling author Donna Grant has been praised for her "totally addictive" and "unique and sensual" stories. She's written more than one hundred novels spanning multiple genres of romance including the bestselling Dark King series that features a thrilling combination of Dragon Kings, Druids, Fae, and immortal Highlanders who are dark, dangerous, and irresistible. She lives in Texas with her dog and a cat.

www.DonnaGrant.com
www.MotherofDragonsBooks.com

facebook.com/AuthorDonnaGrant

instagram.com/dgauthor

bookbub.com/authors/donna-grant

amazon.com/Donna-Grant/e/B00279DJGE

pinterest.com/donnagrant1

CPSIA information can be obtained
at www.ICGtesting.com
Printed in the USA
LVHW011921151021
700575LV00019B/1961